Read and Then Burn This

a novella
by Ryszard Merey

Book II. Fall

A tRaum Book.
Munich, 2024.
Cover font: Zero Liner.

For Valerie.

0

Hands softer than birds.
Yeah.
Women's white hands, the color of arabesques.

1

I heard it before I felt it.

I don't think anyone else heard it; they couldn't when the rifle shot was contained inside my skin. Birds scattered out of the brush, all over in my head. I remember even before the first stab of unbearability, thinking: well, that's that. For everything. Luckily, I had to get off stage right then anyway, and I did somehow, leaning against the back wall in the dark, draping my sweaty self over the Pharaoh's throne. Foundation slid off and blood drained out of my face, milliliter by milliliter.

Juan, the stage manager, hyperventilated over in his short-short shorts.

"Kid, you gotta go! They're about to move this piece and you're in the way."

"I can't," I told him calmly. "My leg's broken."

"Is this a joke? Because it really ain't funny..."

"Really. My leg's broken," I repeated, and he glanced down then. I didn't want to look at my leg myself, after I saw what seeing it did to his face. Even under the perma-tan, the sight mutated his cheeks into two slabs of Stilton cheese.

"Holy shit. ...Manni!" he hissed into the dark, but no answer came and Juan turned back to me and put his hand on my face, more gentle than my ma could've. "Sweetie, you want I call an ambulance?"

I smiled at him.

"I dunno. But I'm going to pass out."

And that's exactly what I did.

2

The first thing I noticed were the beauty of her nails, which is interesting, because there was nothing else about her I found even remotely attractive. Whereas I loved *him* from the first moment—his walk, his sit, his hair, his voice—his name—his profession, which I knew without asking—the entire sum of his being I found worthy of love—but—

She stretched out her hand to me, the right one—I noticed then how well she kept the skin of her hands. They were soft, not a coarse spot on them—she had a tasteful manicure, but entirely natural; no fake nails. I looked at her fingers in mine before our handshake— the beautiful little half-moon of white at the bottom of her cuticle's shell pink.

"You have very nice nails," I said to her. Not as a compliment, though I believed it to be true, but to throw her off the scent. It was a con-compliment, because I hated practically everything else about her. Her nasal voice (harboring the fugitive of a New York accent), her bottle-blonde locks (yes, I'm a hypocrite), that wonderful suit that seemed wasted on a body not designed for designer clothes—the weak jerk-off of a handshake she offered (I cannot *stand* the limpdick way some girls shake your hand)—that overblown gardenia of a name (Valerie Beaumont, it's nice to finally meet you) and most of all her *face*. Yes, it's rude, but I hated her face: broad, creamy, with big grey eyes that reminded me of double quarters resting on two small white saucers— twin overblown irises the color of screws.

Expressionless.

She plunked down next to me.

"Are you painting your nails?"

And I dabbed some more on my pinky, while I pulled my feet up under me.

"Yeah."

"Isn't that whiteout?"

"Uh-huh. I found the bottle here on the coffee table. Sorry, uhm... is it yours? I'll stop wasting it."

She smiled and watched my progress as if it really interested her.

"A well-groomed boy with a lip ring who paints his nails white while watching *My Fair Lady*. Is it safe to say you won't be my next boyfriend?"

At least her personality wasn't a total drag. I laughed.

"I'm a stereotype; I know it."

"It's OK, so am I. WASP princess, it's a pleasure, for sure."

"'Wasp'?"

"We're the debutantes of the cold North."

The tubby deb seemed eager for conversation even over the blare of the TV, so I tried—I don't know why.

"I see. And are you also a fan of musicals? ...Audrey Hepburn was so perfect here. Seriously, that woman deserves to be worshipped. Let's put her on the ten-dollar bill."

Valerie scrunched her face and I stood to open the window; came back, and observed us from above, disconnected, like a scientist watching two hostile chemicals interact in an aberrant and fascinating way.

Taking the bait, she rolled her eyes.

"I can't be the only person who thinks she was so overrated. And musicals are ridiculous. All that dancing and singing in the streets? Come on."

I knew what she was doing—tarrying—she had her hit and was waiting for me to come in with my epee, and my next line should've been to say that dancing and singing in the streets was *beautiful* and that *Burberry's* was ridiculous—you spit on my Bible, and I'll spit on yours, eye for an eye; but I didn't want to start the hostilities first day, so I swiped the bottle from the middle of the table, ready to tackle my right hand and ignore the hell out of her. She asked:

"Are we off on the wrong foot because I dare to not like musicals? ...Want me to do that for you?" Now her gaze fizzled out (somebody's home, but the lights aren't on) and I was still standing with my hands at her eye level.

"Do what?"

"Paint your right hand. It's hard to do it yourself. I know."

Before I could answer, she grabbed my right wrist— as stiff as she seemed, it was a vaguely mothering motion, but a bit like the bad touch, and I was so surprised, my body melted down onto the couch by her side—no conscious shift in my brain from standing to sitting, just a complete release of my muscles. I poured myself out of a highball glass onto the sofa next to her. The woman started to frost my thumb, her eyes screwed up in high concentration while she murmured:

"Wow. You move beautifully. So I guess it's true."

"What... is?"

"That you're a dancer. That's what Michael said."

"More of a dance teacher for now. I'm still recovering from an accident. But yeah."

"A creative person has finally come to this house. That's wonderful. You know, I don't think I have a creative bone in my body."

Relief colored her tone, as if creativity was a malicious disease she was lucky to have never contracted. Almost done with my hand, Valerie raised her face and I found myself making eye contact with her expensive looking pin—it was much preferable to her eyes. I asked:

"And what do you do? Are you a student?"

It seemed unlikely with her fancy clothes, but her age hung somewhere in the precarious region between twenty-two and forty-eight. The corner of her tongue stuck out of her mouth like a tiny piece of moist ribbon, and then she pulled it back in, for emphasis.

"Office. Work."

That's all she said—my hand was done—Henry Higgins and Eliza Doolittle dueled in the background. Valerie got up and smoothed down the renegade wrinkle in an A-line skirt that strained to contain her thighs. I had little trouble imagining her punishing them regularly into submission on a Stairmaster, then confusing them with oversized cappuccinos. Good cop/bad cop—later, it was clear: *That was her, all the way.* The front door opened and I heard my other roommate throw his coat over the hat rack—

"It's too bad." She kept talking and the asymmetry of her lips fascinated me to rudeness. "You're new to Boston, am I correct?"

"I moved here last week, yeah."

"Well, I'd offer to take you around some of the clubs, to go dancing sometime—but you know?" She threw a strand of blonde hair over her shoulder and started to walk out of the living room. "I think dancing might be my least favorite activity in the whole world. I'd even rather do... my taxes."

I stared at her, dumbfounded—Michael poked his head in the door, looking uncertain about the white-out fumes and Rex Harrison's booming voice—

You guttersnipe! You squashed cabbage leaf!

"Uh... good, so you two have met?"

"Yeah." Valerie gave me a little wave and him a mis-placed, flirtatious wink. "You did a good job picking the new roommate, Mike. I really like this one."

Michael looked me a question—*What did you do to piss her off already?*—and I shrugged, glad only that she was gone. In one of those cruel and completely com-monplace visceral first impressions, I judged Valerie as physically unsuitable and artistically bankrupt—worse. An Enemy of Art.

And she didn't have to stick around to convey my first impression on her: a dreadfully vacant Valley fairy.

Beyond the obvious, I've always despised people who lack expression.

3

And *everything* he does drips with expression.

Turn around, turn around, oh please—do it.

I watch him for a good two weeks, subtly maneuvering behind whenever he comes to drop off a lispy student of mine (Taylor), just so I can follow him into the studio and observe him take a seat. The way he does it—letting his body unclench like water; (states shifting from solid, to liquid, to solid again), the perfect angle of his legs when he rests the right ankle on the left knee—I know it—this one is a *dancer*, no mistake.

I love his voice (raspy).

The glow of his name signed in the visitor's register—(Colin A. Savoy—).

What does the "A" stand for?

Adrian. Alfred. Arthur.

I love how he fixes on Taylor whenever they're speaking—him and I have no reason to talk beyond hellos, but when he talks to her (or more likely, her to him), he has an intense way of looking down and studying her face—her mouth—as if this seven-year-old's words are the most important sounds to him—but no, do not tell me he's her father.

He doesn't seem old enough, but it's not a biological impossibility.

Then he looks over at me before he leaves her for the hour and nods a courteous goodbye—flicks hair out of his face—

Straight, sleek, gasoline-colored hair.

Smoke black eyes—*holy hell.*

And the dark angel never speaks to me, only sits off to the side the last five minutes of Taylor's class, shattering my focus. The third week after I first saw him, he comes in again. Class is almost over and one little girl's refusing to try a walkover. I have been spotting the kids for the last forty-five minutes and Kayley's the only one left. I'm trying to talk her into it when he slips in the door, says nothing; lowers his hips, crosses his legs; takes out a book—that I am dying to read now, so that I can innocuously bring up our coincidentally corresponding literary tastes if I ever finally talk to him (I don't actually read or talk to boys) and my brain stubs a toe. Kayley's tiny tin voice brings me back:

"But I'm going to fall. You do it first."

"Yeah, you do it."

The kids raise their voices, and this is a common enough phenomenon. I've noticed that they take every chance they get to make me do a move, until I feel as much a performing monkey as I do their teacher—love it, love it, love it—and glancing over, I see him still reading. Look away.

"Kayley, come on. You already watched everyone else go—just try it, I'm not going to let you fall. Like I showed you."

"Please. One time."

I sigh, stand up, which is when his head rises from his book, as if my movement was a flag, more vital than any sound—*yes, thank you, look at me, look at me.* Swallowing, I walk out to the middle of the floor, stretch my back—raise my fingertips to the ceiling—give Kayley one more glance that says, "Are you watching?" but it's really for him. Then I bend to the floor, slowly. Smell the hardwood's polish as it comes closer to me—(every move most have your everything in it, I always tell the kids—even the simplest ones). My fingertips connect with the sleek wood, grip it, and I balance on my hands, two seconds longer than needed. One leg kicks over; the other—I stand in the bridge, feel the rush of blood to my face, enjoy it—then grip the floor with my toes, clench with my thighs, feel my quads pulling me up while I push off the floor with my hands—(this move is for *you*)—each bone in my spine lines up, drawing my torso like a chain, until I'm on my feet again. Shoulder-blades back—toes gripping the ground— hands like knives.

It's a very hidden language.

Kayley's mouth flops slightly ajar.

"Again."

And it feels good to move, so I do another forward—two walkovers back, then kneel down by the mat, back where I had started.

"Alright. You told me to, and I did it, so no more excuses."

"Do I... have to do them that slow, Ly?"

"No, I did them slow so you could see exactly what to do." Nodding, she puts her little hands up and I help her get into the handstand. "Pull with your thighs... There, that wasn't so hard, right?" Other than a slight collapse in the bridge, it was perfect. Kayley's beaming—parents start trickling in—class is over.

Eight water bottles click open, and I watch the kids torrent out the door. Some of them change in the locker room; most of them don't. Taylor usually does and this is the last class of the day—we close early on Wednesdays—so I grab my things, pull my jacket over the old T-shirt I always wear for teaching—(Wakeful Terrors). He gets up to go wait for Taylor outside, and I turn off the lights.

My calm is in one hundred pieces and I'm on the way to the bathroom when I realize I left my phone in the studio. So I go back, open the door again. Flick the switch. Fluorescents flash up and ooze light over the generous rectangle of hardwood floor. Nureyev's poster wilts behind Helena's tiny desk in the corner, cluttered with paperwork and mementos, sharing a wall full of certificates and trophies and ribbons. The long, long mirror with a few smudges. Mental note to Windex those off tomorrow. I grab my phone off her desk's corner, avoid my eyes in the mirror and take a deep breath.

Shamble back out. Taylor is bouncing around him. "But I have to go to the bathroom." Her whine drifts over and it's so hard to resist turning my head (a minute angle would suffice).

"Well hurry up. Your mom said I have to get you home right after class."

Your mom said, your mom said, are you her dad? She runs towards the changing room and I slink past him, willing myself—do not, do not—and I'm just thinking I've made it when I hear his voice behind my back. The rubber-smelling sprawl of the athletic complex is all around us—airy swoosh of tennis balls being lobbed back and forth on the courts across from our dance studio—muffled thuds as the balls connect with rackets—and no other person.

So he must be addressing *me*.

"Hey. Hang on."

I turn.

The perfect being lies reclined against the wall.

A bead of sweat rolls down my spine, disintegrating as it passes down, nub by nub.

"What?" I grumble— (*You're being a rude asshole!* I scream at me) but he only *smiles* and glancing up, I freeze in that beam like a mouse hypnotized by a mamba. He says:

"Let's go get a cup of coffee. You want to?"

I want to marry you.

"Why?"

Stupefied by his beauty, all I can produce are terse growls that he watches fall out of my face with all the endearing intensity he watches Taylor with.

—and I blush waiting for his response, which makes him smile again, but it's really more like a smirk.

"What. Why. Who. Where. When. Too many questions."

4

Those first weeks were lonely.

Valerie was the only one to use the kitchen besides me, though she never cooked. She'd come home after work, often at seven in the evening as I was steaming broccoli or rice. Stand off to the side, swishing red wine around in a large, globular glass (do people actually do that?) and watch me mutilate food, while making perfectly banal conversation about things I couldn't care less about. Always painfully made up (confusing luxurious product with skill, I suppose), and as many hours as I'd spent under a makeup artist getting ready for stage, I felt I could have thrown her a helpful foundation tip or two. And held my tongue.

I mean, I knew she didn't like me and there was no need to exacerbate that fact, though she seemed to like talking *at me*, something I understood all too well. I'd gone to school with fields of girls like Valerie. Peaking at seventeen, misguidedly superior, falling over their own feet to make you their punch line or their pet. I'd had friends who suffered, but I knew the routine. Ignore them until it soaks through that we are existing on different planes. Cue the Labyrinth. *You have no power over me.*

But she was a dedicated lurker—a loyal shadow. I was peeking into the oven at my fish fillets one night when I felt her presence behind me, dangerously close, like our old basset hound Daisy. Right underfoot—*why the hell is she getting so close to me?*

I stepped back sharply, as if I hadn't heard the tread

of her stupid polished shoes—felt my ass bump into her (my legs were so much longer than hers; I must've hit her somewhere in the chest), acid tongued: "Oh sorry, *excuse me.* Didn't see you there," but she didn't step back, sort of lurched against me—her hands steadied the disorientation on my lower waist. One of her fingers caught in my belt, nail seared through my shirt, and I arched my back as if I had touched something dangerously hot. My extreme reaction was embarrassing to us both, so I stayed by the stove, pretending to check the rice, while my blush subsided.

She went over to the table and gently collapsed on one of the chairs, and once it was all done, I loaded up my plate with food and sat next to her. Let her judge my cooking. Option two was taking my plate and eating in my room.

"Mmm. Mmm. Mmm. Your dinner tonight looks especially wholesome. Is that another crowd-pleaser from *The Joys of the Anorexic Kitchen?*"

"This is actually one of my favorites from *Anorexic Meals for One.*" I looked up—joining her in a bad joke was easier than ignoring her completely, but her eyes seemed even duller than normal. Hazed, and very sad. The food caught in my throat.

"Uhm, is everything alright?"

"Sure. Just drank a little too much."

Not surprising. Sometimes, I saw her drinking in the living room at night—sometimes even an entire bottle of red wine alone, which I didn't understand— isn't drinking bottles of alcohol in one sitting something alcoholics or Very Sad people do? Didn't she have a boyfriend? Not my problem. Still, her face had such a miserable color, so I stood up and poured her a glass of water—gave her a sleeve of saltines from my side of the cupboard. I'm no expert with drunk people, but my brother Russell used to swear by toast when he was hungover—

"Crackers?" She ripped open the package with suspicion. "What are these supposed to do?"

"I think they help soak up the bad stuff in your stomach. Cause they're dry. ...Rough day?"

Valerie tossed four crackers down the hatch and I watched the top of her smart blazer get snowed by a blizzard of crumbs. When she stifled a rather juicy belch against the back of her hand, I hoped my shudder wasn't too obvious.

"Awful. Doesn't help that Michael had to harass me about the rent, right as I was getting ready to unwind in the living room. I'm really starting to regret that car."

"What car?"

"You know... the Beamer outside?" Her rainy eyes sliced me with disdain, like, why even bother with financially draining status symbols if the dolts around you are too clueless to seethe?

I babbled. "Oh I didn't notice. I mean, I'm not really into cars, so I don't notice them unless they're really out there, you know, like a tank... or a Hummer... or something."

A ghost of a smile came to her lips.

"Yeah, I bet you like a nice hummer."

My eyebrow arched and I was seriously annoyed, but didn't want to come across as overly sensitive.

Blotches and stains spread on her cheeks, from the wine she had drunk and the heat from the oven rising up in the kitchen. Valerie took a piece of broccoli from my plate and I stiffened—I'll hug anyone, but food is another realm— She tossed the sprig into her mouth, gnawing it like cud while she looked out the window.

"I'm sorry—I shouldn't have said that. It's the red wine talking, really."

"Hey, don't worry about it."

But please don't reach into my plate again, or I'll freak the freak out.

You'd have thought she had a direct tap into my brain. Valerie poised her pretty hand over my food and absent-mindedly picked through it—that's it. There was no way I was going to be able to finish my dinner tonight, so I stretched my hand out and started eating saltines too.

"Yeah." Her fingers lazily settled over a broccoli head and she pinched it to death, like the squishy body of an overcooked tick. "I don't blame you if you can't finish this. Ly, you want me to give you a cooking lesson sometime? You eat the same terrible boiled crap, night after night."

"Thanks, but my ma already tried that. I failed miserably. Anyway, there's only about five things on the planet that I can eat and not have my stomach go berserker. What you could do is invent a pill I can take every day and not have to eat another meal again."

"What did eating ever do to you?" She raised the fat stomach of her glass and started the wine swishing again.

Maybe I could've tried to explain my food thing to

her, but I had a feeling she'd just use it as ammo. Better to fire first instead.

"Does any of that actually *do* anything, or is it just a Marlene Dietrich prop?"

The grande dame trapped me with her wolf-trap eyes. "Yes, it does do something, Mr. Skeptical. It helps the wine breathe. Red wines generally need to be aerated before you can fully enjoy their flavor—especially the younger ones. But I guess you're not into wine?"

I'm not old enough to 'be into' wine.

Is what I didn't say.

"Not really."

"It's a shame, a California boy. But you've got time to get into wine, get into food. Into all sorts of things. This is a really nice young Australian cab. You want a sip?"

She pressed her glass under my nose and, sensing that she wouldn't take no for an answer and not wanting to make the situation weirder, I took a sip. The last time I had tried a red, it was some nasty cheap stuff at my uncle's house one holiday back—sour and metallic, like licking rust with a faint aftertaste of sick. This, however, was a pleasant surprise, reminding me of blackberries and velvet (if velvet had a taste), and I enjoyed the hot trail of it down into my throat. Gave her back the glass.

"Hey. That's actually, pretty nice."

"See? You've gotta trust me." She took another sip. "You've only got one life to live. *Got to try everything.* Right?"

Valerie winked at me then. Her open eye glinted like an obscene conspiracy and I wondered if she was just drunk, or trying to send me a secret signal, but hell if I knew what it was.

5

Colin and I spend that first afternoon walking around. We drop Taylor off after getting her a bagel, then go and buy coffees, and I know I shouldn't be fritzing my stomach but get one anyway. I want to be agreeable and normal to him, though I notice how his lip curls at the atrocious amount of sugar and milk I avalanche into my cup. He drinks his black, which I find very attractive and virile, and we walk out on the promenade along the Charles—this is when I find out that Taylor is not his daughter.

"You thought she was?" He grins. "I love my nieces, but I don't think that's going to be my life." Taylor is his oldest sister's daughter, and this sister happens to be going through a rough divorce. "I'm trying to help her out a little, drop Taylor off for her activities when I have time—but I won't soon. I'll be too busy with a show. Yeah, I dance too. Are you surprised?"

From the first second I saw you, I knew you couldn't be doing anything else.

Is not what I tell him.

"Not at all." I look away when I say it and he turns to me.

"Sorry, what was that?"

"I said, I'm not surprised that you dance. Not at all."

He stops then, taking a sip of coffee, and fixes his eyes on my face while I say those three words—*not at all*—. Fixates on my mouth, like he is reading something crucial out of me, experiencing the meaning not only with his ears, but his sight, eyes to my lips, which makes me shiver and, oddly, I think of my roommate Valerie in that moment—except never do I feel more invisible than when she looks at me; which is the entire opposite of this—his gaze is inquisitive—and his irises go into me deep and radiant, dark opals lit up with a secret inner light. I sink in them, getting consciously *wooed* and he says:

"That's better. I should have told you earlier, but you really can't turn away when you say something to me."

What, what, what?

"...W-what?" I blather.

"What I mean to say is, I'm hard of hearing. It's pretty severe—but the hearing in my right ear is much better than my left. It's very strange, but I find your voice easy to understand for some reason. Most other people, I would've had to tell them by now. That I read lips."

Blithering all over:

"Oh... I had... no idea... so should I...?"

"It's fine. You don't have to talk louder or overemphasize words. But either walk on my right side when we speak, or it helps if you face me so I can see your mouth move and your expressions."

Moving to his other side, I dent my not-yet-empty coffee cup and he says:

"I'm sorry. I should've said something earlier. You've probably been wondering why I stare at you so intensely when you talk."

No... I liked it.

"No, I mean... I noticed, that... you... do that... but I thought... it meant..."

He saves me from saying something potentially daft. "Anyway, if you've been wondering, now you know.

But I've been wondering too if you're ever going to tell me?"

"Tell you... what, exactly?"

"What an obviously talented dancer like you is doing, killing precious time teaching seven-year-olds. Unless that is the sole reason you moved all the way here from California, you said? In which case, my apologies."

No. But I don't know how to explain the mystery of the leg, and how I'm waiting for another sign, to put me back on track. When I told my ma I wouldn't be auditioning for schools but moving to Boston to follow up on this studio position I had gotten through an old troupe contact, I thought she was going to detonate.

"You're delaying school? But why Boston?"

"Because I need a change."

"But you can't quit now!"

"I'm not quitting. I'm taking a break."

"But why so far?"

"Because I want to see snow."

Every reason I gave was random—but then it was all random. Colin looks at me now.

"So why Boston?"

"Because I wanted to live somewhere that got snow."

"You could've moved to New York."

"I didn't want that much anonymity. New York is so—huge, like it doesn't need another single person more. Definitely not me. But someday, I'm sure I'll get there. Who doesn't dream of dancing in a New York show?"

He drinks his drink while I pretend to drink mine.

"And how are you going to get into shows if you're

not dancing seriously? You know, Ly, by your mid-twenties even, you'll start getting more injuries. I'm twenty-six, and I've already started developing problems with my back. And then I've had this Achilles tendon issue in my left leg for years. You'll have all the time in the world to teach or choreograph when you're older, but right now, your body is in perfect shape. May I ask how old you are?"

"Nineteen," I mumble, wishing I was older or a liar. Damn, did he say twenty-six? I feel like an utter *kid*, but rather than putting him off, my answer concurs with his point.

"...See what I mean? Listen, you're a good teacher, but it's obvious that you belong on stage. It's none of my business, I know, but it seems like... such a waste."

Turning colors, I mumble into my lapels.

"Come on. You've never even seen me dance, Colin."

"Why do you think I've been coming to Helena's so often? This is exactly why I wanted to talk to you. I've been watching you at the studio. You *walk* with more presence than many dancers exhibit on stage. You have a lot of energy—a lot of poise. I asked Helena about you, but she didn't know anything. She said an old colleague of hers who'd moved to California had vouched for you, and she was satisfied with how things are going, but that you're pretty closed-mouthed."

Because there wasn't much to say, but I give him a recap now. *Nothing* else ever mattered to me—and then, there I was at this crucial time, laid up in the hospital. I couldn't move. My dance friends were coming in to visit—all going to auditions, dancing for admissions panels—and for years and years and years, I had never let myself go, always thinking it was so important. Don't let down your guard—don't slack—don't rest for a minute—other than my family, I didn't know anybody or anything outside of my company. That's why my leg broke, really, because that show too—

"You broke your leg?" he asked.

"It snapped. On stage, during a show. One second, I had landed the aerial and next, it just broke like a matchstick. Even that was my fault, because I had ignored the pain for so long. Acted like if *I* said my leg was hurting and stepped out, I would be letting everyone down. And now, here I was—physical therapy, the whole thing. I was completely unable to move and *it didn't matter*. My whole world was moving on without me."

"But people get injuries all the time," Colin says. "I had to have an operation on my tendon five years ago. I was out for months. It happens. It hurts to see everything move on so effortlessly without you, but you have to power through it."

"Sure... I know. It's just. The timing was so... It was a massive fracture—absolutely no movement for eight weeks. Even worse, I knew it was my fault—improper nutrition—stress—there was a school up in San Francisco I had wanted to audition for and the date slipped by—and I got pretty depressed. I was in therapy for a while."

"And did you dance on it?"

"Yeah, that was another problem. I couldn't resist forcing it. And it wasn't properly healing, so I had to keep going back to the doctor. Still in pain, still not healing and that's when they said I risked permanently injuring my leg and losing a dance career altogether. That scared the hell out of me, because I don't know how to do ANYTHING else, so I thought then, I need to get away. Take it totally easy. I got this job."

"And how is your leg today?"

"As far as I know, completely fine. Except now, well... I don't know what to do. I figure, I could start auditions, maybe go to a school—but I'm a little freaked. I try to keep myself in shape, dance regularly at Helena's, but it feels like the critical window has closed."

"Maybe not quite yet. Listen, this may not be New York, but there are some excellent schools here. You must know about the Conservatory. Have you considered applying there?"

I laugh glumly.

"Yeah. Right. Like I could ever make it in there. *Nobody* makes it in there."

Colin stops then and holds out his hand.

"So now you know the full reason for why I wanted to talk to you. Nobody, from the class of 2005. Nice to meet you."

I'm ready to fall over. And that's when he tells me that the school's head of modern dance, a woman he calls Marichka, is his mentor, and remains a close personal friend, and that he could potentially get me an audition for the next term—a school I would've sold any part of my body or soul to get into. The air is cold, but not wet. Far off, a dog sniffs a maple tree, then pisses it down, little enthusiasm. The dog's owner looks bored as well. Colin stands next to me and I nestle my coffee cup into the grass—

"Quick, what color is this move?" I do a handstand off the top of the bench—hold it, taking the world in upside down. Him, the man, and the dog and the pissed-down tree—the world takes me back, until I push myself over, feel the seat of the bench with my toes, ease myself down facing the wrong way. Colin sits the wrong way next to me—

"You are very limber. And surprisingly strong. Did you ever do..."

"Gymnastics? Started with it, but liked dance better."

"The move is red, by the way."

"I agree. Well, orange-red, but close enough. An arabesque?"

"White."

"Grand jeté?"

"Silver."

We are not synaesthetes, but we almost make it through every move, until my torso wavers like flames in a wind and Colin looks concerned.

"Are you...?"

"I'm fine, but I just now realized that I've had basically nothing to eat today. Do you mind if we get some food?" We start to walk, with me on his right, and I'm grateful that he seems to have forgotten about the audition talk. I want to make him forget further. "So, I'm sorry, but I've never known someone with a... hearing problem... before. Have you had it since birth?"

"No. It developed when I was eleven. I contracted

meningitis. But before I tell you the whole fascinating story, we have to decide which way we're going, so where do you want to go? What do you like to eat?"

I smile at him. "Absolutely nothing."

"Uhm?"

The last person to want food is me—that's how disoriented I've gotten in his presence—so we leave while I explain the holy trinity of foods I can consume (fish, rice, vegetables), leaving out the more intricate rules of combinations and appearances, and he suggests a sushi place downtown (but not even rice and fish will go down). I'm too nervous, so I just watch him—he is a pit—finishes his food, finishes my food, and we talk all over, about ex-shows and dream roles; our mutual hate of Morrissey, adoration of *Chicago* and MJ's genius, until I like him too much, and by the time we're done eating, I'm dead sure this is the best date I've ever been on.

—I just don't know if he's on a date too.

Though he picks up the whole bill.

A weak fall shower starts outside and he offers to drive me home—I note it, a real gentleman, but the gentleman doesn't press his advantage, only strides next to me, narrow-hipped, long-legged. Girls check him every time we stand to cross, bad sign. He seems oblivious to all females, good sign. And I stay on his right, feeling so positively *mortal.*

Too soon, we're sitting in his car outside of my apartment. I watch the dreamy pulse of Mike's big-screen TV out the second-floor window and, through our windshield, those breaks in the gray-purple overcast, sprinkled with a faint-burning field of sulphuric stars.

"Do you live alone?" he asks me.

"No. I've got some roomies."

"Ahh. You're all friends?"

"No, I mean, we found each other online. I think they were desperate to fill the room, because they accepted me in an email and a short phone interview. There's Mike, going into banking. There's this girl, Mira, who's a graduate student. Then this woman, Valerie. She's a total weirdo."

"A weirdo, you say. How so?"

I can't explain what makes Valerie odd to me. It's too nuanced. "Maybe it's just me. If you ever meet her, you'll see."

"Alright."

He asks me for my phone and I listen to him punch his number into it. He says:

"I won't be picking Taylor up for a while. My schedule is changing starting next week, so I might not see you at the studio. If you ever change your mind about the audition, call me."

"OK."

I take the phone from him and am about to get out of the car, but I want to say thank you for the ride home, for the meal, for the nice night, so I turn around. I want to be *polite*.

"Colin—"

"Yeah?"

Heart pounding. I put my mouth close to his ear, pretending I have to, because it's softdark and he can't read my face.

"Thanks for the nice night and the dinner and uhh, well... I wanted to ask... Well, what if... well, if I could call you... about something other than the audition?"

I'm bent over, looking down. He leans forward. Our first physical contact is his lips on mine and I have to struggle to not press him into me. He seems amused by it.

"Call me for anything, Ly."

6

Herbal tea is my fallback for when I can't eat, and my stomach was twisted into a fist after that kiss in his car. I thought maybe a shower might have a calming effect, so I finished the tea, then took a towel from my room—our bathroom has no lock, but the implicit rule is that a closed door means stay out. I wasn't sure how many of the others were home. TV noises hummed from the living room, so I figured Michael was watching a game. Then I was in the shower—they had an old free-standing porcelain tub with the shower curtain that you could pull around, and I felt safe, like in a secret booth, and the water was good there. It came out hot and strong and my muscles unclenched while I hummed a nocturne my beginning ballet class was dancing to, thinking back on the afternoon, on talking to him—our dinner—

The door opened. I saw the steam over the shower curtain swell. Disturbed heat billowed around in moist, chalky clouds.

"I'm in here, so only if it's an emergency," I called out, not particularly enjoying the prospect of someone squatting down on the john while I was in the shower. Valerie's reedy voice cut through the steam. Why was I not surprised?

"I know you're in here. I have a question."

"Uh... OK. I'm almost done. Can I just come meet you in the living room?"

She didn't answer. Slippers scluffscluffed against tiles, then a hand gripped a handful of steamed plastic and flung the shower curtain open. I stood there, buck-nude and perhaps not as shocked as I should've been—be it the locker room, studio or stage, dancers are used to putting their bodies on display. The bad tongues even say that we live for it. Still, if I was expecting some shock from her end, it wasn't coming. She looked me over appreciatively, lacking all embarrassment. As if I were a picture on her wall.

We stared at each other. The hot water ran—I was dripping, wet—she was totally clad, up to her neck in another fancy designer suit, like every day I'd seen her so far. Wayward spray darkened her shirt's white collar. That night, her blonde hair was drawn back in a chignon, and she held the remote control, of all things, out to me.

"Can you tell me which one of these buttons starts the DVD player?"

I took a moist finger and gently poked towards the lower half of the control, not wanting to wetten it.

"It's that blue button."

"Thanks. I've been pressing every damn button on this thing for the last ten minutes."

"Well I guess you didn't press the blue one."

She wouldn't move.

"Can I finish my shower now?" I asked dryly and she gave me a long stare, spanning a good three seconds before she closed the curtain again. The last thing I saw was her thin lopsided mouth bent into a mocking smile.

"Look at *you*."

Those three words made me more red than any other aspect of her performance thus far.

7

Your father was a wonderful dancer. That's where you got it from. You didn't get it from me.

My ma told me a lot about my dad growing up, showed us pictures of him all the time and secretly, but only very very secretly, I thought he was a babe. I wish I looked like him—that's my brother Russell though. He got my father's sharp James Dean looks. I have my mother's flat, old-world face. Her pale eyes (but no blond hair). People called my features "delicate" and hers "handsome" (not pretty). She'd come home from the plant office rubbing her eyeballs from glaring at the screen all day and we tried to stay out of her way, make it a little easier on her. It's not that she was rigid, but she was already worried about what growing up without a dad might do to Russell.

And what dancing too much might do to me.

Unfortunately, I wasn't born loving to dance, only

with an inclination to be good at it, which my mother decided to develop, for my own benefit. And I let her, never fighting, because whatever I was at school, with other kids (who concerned me about as much as the wind patterns on Mars), or with my brother and his friends, when I danced, I knew I was worthy of attention. It was the only time I was even remotely extraordinary.

The one thing I resented was the discipline's level of encroachment—summer, winter, weekends, friends—I had nothing else—and our shared fixation was starting to make both me and my ma neurotic.

I remember the Saturday afternoon that marked the end of an era. It was desperately hot. I had been dancing the same piece for her in the basement over and over. My brother and some kids were outside eating popsicles and playing under the hose and, wanting to join them, I put it out to her. I thought, if I make this perfect, she will have to let me go—and I knew that I could do that—like the arrogance of a sun rising, I felt the perfection of each move—tighter than a tourniquet, knowing there was no flaw in my movements her eyes would ever detect. The only human sound above my labored breathing was the soft reverberation of her "again" each time I got to the end of the routine, in another language in which I knew a handful of secret words—and I got up each time dutifully, to rewind the tape to the beginning of the song— reached the end again. This is how we talked to each other. Her "again" my "hmmm" "again" "hmmm" while I unraveled—from an eager kid, to a mendicant, to a thrall.

"Ma, I want to go outside..."

Barred ground-level windows coated in dust threw down their golden slats all around and I twirled in them while listening to Russell shrieking with neighbor kids ten feet above my head. They trampled the back lawn's dusty grass to death, while the water of the hose slapped against the panes, ineffectually lapping at the dust. My mom noticed me looking up, so she turned up the sound, thinking I was getting distracted. She didn't want the noises of ordinary summer life invading my ascent to genius.

"One more time. You need to watch it at the end. You go into the turn on the fourth beat, not the second. You missed that twice now."

"Ma..."

I danced on, knowing she had made that up.

"Can I go now?"

"Just one more time."

"You said that before."

"You said you would have it down by now. It wasn't perfect."

"Yes, it was. And I'm tired."

Her thick accent made any sarcasm double piercing. "Do it anyway, Lysandrze. You are too young to be tired."

But I really was—covered in the light, unsmelly sweat of kids, and bored. I hated her then, for crashing my sanctuary, for turning music into a mere solution bathing me. I remember—that one last dance in front of my mother, the final one I wanted so much to not finish. Each chord developed a reek about it. Each twist of my ankles, wrists, smelled of a subtle grief that enveloped my body, not unidentical to the feeling I got after I masturbated. My face hottened (would she know what I was thinking about?). The dance inverted on itself. Her tortoiseshell-framed glasses glinted on her high-boned face while she watched with a blank, inert intensity, without any seeming interest in my moves, but as if my dance was the key to my soul. Then I stopped mid-leap, a human stag frozen by a hunter's gun, and bounded to the tape deck. Tore the tape out of it.

"I won't finish it, I won't do it again! It was fine and you're ruining it!"

"L..."

"You're ruining it! I hate this, I hate it!" Getting drunk off the situation, I screamed it so loud the kids outside stopped hosing and pressed their candywet faces to the panes. My grandma Yvonne came shuffling down, a woman even tinier than my tiny mom. She was my grandmother from my father's side who had moved to our city after my father had died in the car crash—what in god's name—she sorted me out with a backhand that almost made me sit on the ground. She wore pants like men sit mounts and slapped harder than a horse's kick and I blinked back tears. Russ used to say, whatever you do, watch her LEFT hand (she was left-handed).

"I don't want to see you crying, Lys, you better not be crying after that production. Are you crying?"

"No ma'am."

"Good. Now what the botheration?"

"She won't let me go outside." I cradled my cheek. Shame unfurled hot petals in me. Eleven was too old to get slapped by your grandma. Russell and his friends snickered outside and my grandmother glanced over at my ma.

"Is that what this racket is about? Then go, for crissakes. Get out of here."

Skittering like an insekt up out of the basement before either of them could change their minds and the last thing I heard was my grandmother's smoker-croak: "Ada, you've *got* to marry again. You're driving him and yourself both crazy, and the boys need a father. In another few years, they'll be unmanageable."

My grandma said it often after that. She came over practically every afternoon (to babysit) and every Thursday night (for chicken pot pie), and my ma started going out again, to interview potential fathers. I used to love watching her get ready for her dates. She'd put on a boat-necked sheath dress, rub perfume on the back of her wrists, a dab behind the ears. Her toughness melted away and she became sweet Doris Day out on the prowl. Then if the guy ever got far enough to eat a family dinner at our house (Pork-chops, mint sauce; can't eat anything with the (possibly) future Rock Hudson sitting across me, nerves, nerves!), she'd ask us afterwards, all nervous, What did you think, boys? She'd take off the beautiful ring my dad had given her, and do the dishes, up to her elbows in neon rubber gloves and Russell harpooned her boyfriends down sulkily (he was a *douche*), while I nursed deep and indelible crushes on them.

"That's enough, Russell! You'll never like anyone, so I shouldn't even bother asking you. And what did you think? ...Lysandrze?"

Oooh, loaded question, Ma. He might want to steal your boyfriend, 'cause—

"You're such a little *fag*, Ly." Russell had been telling me long before I even suspected it myself. He'd sneer it at me, usually when I danced around the house or was stretching downstairs and "Shut up!" I'd screech back at him, not that I even knew what that word meant at seven, eight, and nine, only that it must be bad because he'd mouth it at me softly, careful so Ma wouldn't hear. As if only he knew my true, mysterious wickedness. That I was in a highly forbidden state of being. And as the good kid, I didn't *want* to be mysterious, nor wicked—unlike my brother, I embraced the reheated leftovers of my ma's childhood spirituality: I never cursed; believed in love and marriage; and avoided the dual temptations of *Beverly Hills 90210* and *Beavis and Butthead* as possible catalysts to moral rot—

Which is why I was so relieved when I finally unlocked the mysteries of the word sometime in late grade school.

Oh.

Being a f-g just means you like boys.

It seemed pretty harmless, unlike being an asshole (Russell's specialty); still, fantasizing about the cutie who danced next to you in intermediate ballet was apparently worse than setting trash cans on fire and being a bully at school. Now my ma had a new fear—and I had to endure many a Sunday afternoon down in the sweaty basement of the King of Kings, nodding off to Ms. Creacy's creamy tidbits about Jesus helping the dispossessed. However, not only did church and Bible study utter-ly fail to make me feel guilty about admiring boys in tight jeans, it also introduced me to Jude: a pale, rebellious-mouthed kid with the most fire-soaked sullen eyes I'd ever seen. He'd sit next to me in class and whisper the kind of hip, heretical things I didn't even dare say *in my brain*, let alone out loud. Like how he was going to convert to Judaism as soon as he turned eighteen, just to tick his mom off (a real Bible-*humper*, is what he called her)—how he couldn't *concentrate* on being good and chaste while being forced to stare for hours at a sexy half-naked man nailed to a cross. Two years older than me, I thought he was plain radical, which is why I asked him to be my first kiss out in the church parking lot while we waited for our moms to pick us up in their sedans.

You ever kiss anyone, Jude?
My girlfriend, sure.
You mind if I kiss you?
That's cool, Ly. I'll do it for the experience.

Jude was my only non-dance friend growing up, so when he quit church, I did too and my ma hit the roof. But I was faithfully attending practices. I was in youth companies, making good, and we had a nice don't ask don't tell percolating, until one day when I was helping her fix dinner and I told her of this audition I was thinking about and right between the "Can you get me the tenderizer?" and "Do you really want to work with Benny after all those problems you had with him in *Coppélia?*" she started nattering about these *diseases* and how scared she was for me. With his impeccable timing, Russ showed up just then. (She's talking about

AIDS, Ly. God made it to punish people like you—Russell, I'm having a serious conversation with your brother and that's a despicable thing to say, so get out!) and I sat at the kitchen bar, feeling my spine solidify with embarrassment.

"Ma, stop, please. I'm not into... *that*... anyway. It's *gross.*"

That being tab a, slot b.

She gave me an odd look, like she didn't totally believe me, but neither of us were prepared to bandy around grotesque words like "condom" and "anal sex," and how could I convince my ma at fifteen that I truly wasn't interested anyway? My mind was elsewhere. Dancing preoccupied all of my need for movement, expression—the physique. I jerked off the way people floss their teeth—nightly and without fuss, and when I did think of something involving reciprocity—sweating? Groaning? Ugh. Please no. I wanted sex *romantic.* I imagined it with an unusually good-looking boy who *loved me*, in a bed with clean sheets—just kissing and petting. You know. Nothing disgusting.

An attitude that did not endear me to all the dancer boys who wanted indiscriminate backstage gropefests, and so the closest I came to having someone was this one guy Mitchell, but he wasn't honest with himself or anybody, which is why we didn't care for each other and why I could only call him a demi-boyfriend. Still, sadly, my only real experience. Some bio project. We were meeting at his house twice a week. He was a dusky, tall kid with a freckled nose and a boxer's body—gold eyes—factions of girls were committing suicide over his face. And then, with our bio books splayed out and our notes cramping the whole island of his family's modern kitchen, it was a tremendously surprise seduction.

We went to his room where he licked me down and French kissed me and told me how *dead I was* if I ever told anyone and I lay in a complacent, blank ecstasy saying sure, sure, I won't tell, because he was masculine and a vacuum couldn't hold a candle to this guy's mouth. And since I had him to myself, in a suburban bed with (almost) clean flannel sheets, I figured I had met most of my perfect–first-time requirements.

And tried very hard to not fall in love with him.

He laid down the rules the first day: above all, no penetration, because THAT is gay. He was reassured when I told him I'm not into that either. So we just stroked each other a lot, which was nice, and sometimes, he asked me to do things to him, though he preferred giving, and then our bio project ended and I had no reason to go over to his house anymore, nor did he invite me again. Whenever I saw him in school, he'd be walking around with his girlfriend and his husky buddies, too high on the ladder to see me, while I'd laugh inside, feeling sorry for him, because I could still hear his voice—*You won't tell, right? You won't tell?* he'd murmur in my ear, all vulnerable, and sexed-up, and glum with the despair of a poseur.

Yeah, I thought in the halls, I know what's up your alley and I don't care.

The whole affair lasted less than three weeks.

8

Colin invited me for Sunday dinner at his house.

It was Sunday morning and I was space-cadeting, drinking Lemon Zinger and writing his name in the margins of the morning paper after my crossword savvy had reached full saturation. In cursive, admiring its shimmer. Colin Alexander Savoy, Colin Alexander Savoy, Colin Alexander Savoy. Still writing it when Valerie came into the kitchen, toweling her neck (back from a run?). She poured herself a glass of her fancy mineral water and looked over at me.

"What's up with you? You look like you just won the lottery."

"Better. This guy I'm... kind of seeing... invited me to dinner tonight."

"Oooh. I didn't know you have a boyfriend."

"We only recently met, so not my boyfriend." (I don't think.)

She sat down.

"Is it a romantic dinner at his place?"

"No. It's at his parents' house. I guess he eats with them sometimes, on Sunday."

"Where do they live?"

"He texted the address, but I don't know the street. Maybe you know it?"

"Let me see. I might."

I showed her the address on my phone and her eyes narrowed into steely slits.

"One of my exes used to live right around from here. This is on Beacon Hill..."

"OK?" I didn't know her well enough yet to realize my gaff right then, but Beacon Hill meant nothing to me. Valerie scowled.

"It's only one of the best neighborhoods, if not the best, in Boston. Well." Her voice went sour. "*I guess you don't waste any time.*"

"What is that supposed to mean?"

"Nothing. Anyway, take the Green Line to Park Place. This street is one block north from the Commons. Do you have anything decent to wear?"

"He told me it was a casual family dinner at home."

She laughed then and pet my head like I was a kid.

"Listen, Ly. For these people, it's never just dinner at home—take it from me. You've got to be careful. They're going to be judging you. Watching your every move. You don't want to make a bad impression or give them the wrong idea. Or in your case—" Her laugh was crisp and brutal. "—the *right* idea. Remember, Boston is a tad more... plutocratic than what you were probably used to in California. People here can be more unforgiving."

"So what should I do?" I whispered. I hadn't given much thought to Colin's family before. He himself was rather casual—he talked casual; and though he drove a nice car, dressed well, tipped high, and had what my ma might have called "class," it hadn't occurred to me that he might be socially above me. Only aesthetically, mentally, and dance-technically.

Now I had a whole heretofore unconsidered realm to worry about, and I imagined his family glaring at me through monocles, staring me down as I stepped into their hall for the first time. Analyzing my clothes, hair, mannerisms, speech. Even the dog. All monocles. I glanced at his name again in the margins of the paper, and what had seemed like a harmlessly beautiful name moments ago now had the portentous ring of a lordling who had *just* managed to escape a West Point education.

I must've looked flipped, because Valerie started to snicker at me.

"It's not an invitation to a beheading. I just thought you should be warned to dress, you know. Appropriately. Maybe take out the lip ring? Oh and. *Don't wear nail polish.*"

Since the invitation was for four (apparently, Boston dinners start early on Sunday), I was agonizing in front of my closet by one. I showered, shaved, called my friend Trischa back in LA to squeal (dinner—in his house—meeting his family!); then clad myself in the most inoffensive and benign outfit I could put together. A pressed white dress shirt. Black slacks, black blazer. Then I moved into the bathroom, put on a touch of cologne and waxed my hair into a structure not quite like I'd rolled out of bed—but as if it'd been agitated by a well-controlled breeze. Despite her warning, the lip ring stayed, but I swapped in the thinnest, most unobtrusive silver band I had. Inspecting myself, I happily concluded that I looked like an extra from *Dead Poets Society* and went out into the hall. Pulled on my dress shoes—

Valerie had been lazing around in the living room since the morning and, when she heard me in the hall, she called out.

"Hey, you leaving?"

"Yeah."

My hand was on the doorknob when she came over, still in her exercise clothes.

"Wait a minute. Let me see you." I turned around and she walked up to me—didn't stop walking until she was right in front of me, and I stepped back, though there was nowhere to go, just up against the wall. I stepped into the corner. *I need air!* Like those times when I cooked in the kitchen and she moved around right behind me, closer than a dog and always vaguely underfoot; she had that loathy habit some have of completely ignoring your bubble and coming too close to you. She was in mine now, scanned me up and down, then finally stepped back.

I exhaled.

"Well? You're the society pages expert, so do I have to change, or is this fine?"

Valerie reached out with both hands and almost stopped my breath. For a paranoid second, I was sure she would throttle me, but her fingers stopped on my collar—undid the top button of my shirt—opened it at the neck.

Her pinky brushed my throat—

I swallowed.

"*Very fine.*" Was all she said. Her eyes were flat.

I thought of the word *crucifixion.*

I stumbled out the door.

9

I'm walking up the escalator at Park Place when I realize I don't have a gift for my hosts, so I stop at a delicatessen close to the T station and browse for a while. The lady is helpful and I get them a nice box of chocolates, trying not to fret too much about the price, then walk out and cut across Boston Common. The State House looms across the way, its gold dome refracting in the dreary greylight, and I can see for myself now that this area is one ritzy neighborhood. His family lives on W_____ Street and when I walk up to the house, again I have to think of Henry Higgins' Winpole address. The house stands in a line of town houses—a tooth in a line of well-kept teeth, with a wrought iron railing leading up five steps to an imposing and ornate door. I ring the bell and Colin is the one who lets me in.

"Hey there." He looks happy to see me, and I get a little stupid, as I still do when we meet.

"I didn't know what to bring." I hand him the package and he tells me that I didn't need to bring anything. After Valerie's little warning, I want to pull him outside for a thirty-second briefing on how I should act with his possibly aristocratic and bigoted family, but he pulls me in instead. I take off my shoes and—

"Your apartment is amazing," I whisper.

"It's my parents' apartment. But thanks."

A banister twists above our heads, corkscrewing up, up, all the way to the sky—at least three stories, but maybe four, with an old-fashioned skylight at the very top, raining down an amber, muted light. The floor under our feet is checkered black-white tile—we're in an Escher draft—leading narrow and long to the back, where I see a kitchen. In it, an older woman and a younger are working together—both have aprons on, their hair up. The older woman has black hair still—she's short and striking and now I know where Colin got his looks, if not his height. She wipes her hands on a kitchen towel and rushes out to meet us. The extreme grace of her movements makes me wonder if she used to dance. Her body is an efficient and beautiful structure and I reach out to shake her hand, but she surprises me by hugging me instead.

"I'm Hana, and you must be Ly. Ly? Am I saying that right?"

I smile at her. "Close enough."

In school they said Lys like *lies*. Anyone who wanted to aggravate me would innocently pronounce it *lice*. My youth company, friends and family dropped the 's' and always said Ly, like *Lee*—some people, like my grandma, went with *lease*—only my ma ever used my full name, every time. She didn't approve of others shortening it, and would stridently correct school admin, doctors, and anyone who mispronounced it or dared to Anglicize it to Lysander. (I had long felt it was a lost battle.) Colin himself says *Lee*. He asked me to teach him the full version, the way my mother would say it, then gave up and settled on this corruption. I don't mind. His mother goes on.

"Colin told me your family is from Poland."

"Well, my mom. Everyone else is Californian, born and raised."

"Ahh, my sister moved over to Cupertino not long ago. ...So do you know Polish?"

"Just a few words, really. My mom hasn't been back for so long that she says she could not speak it that well herself anymore."

"That makes sense. My extended family all live in Seoul, but I'm so embarrassed, having forgotten all my Korean, that I never do go visit. Oh well, Colin travels enough for all of us—has he told you he's even danced in Krakow?"

"Not specifically, but I'm jealous. Until I came here, I'd never been anywhere but Southern California."

She smiles warmly. "Well, your career is just getting started. I'm sure you'll get to see many places too."

I follow her into the kitchen and meet Colin's younger sister, Deborah. His older sister Hannah (my student Taylor's mother) will not make it for today's dinner. Deborah smiles and waves at me, standing at a marble countertop, breading trout ("He told us that you like fish.") and Colin gives his mother my package. She thanks me for it, hugging me again, and then he takes my hand. Neither his mother nor sister take an especial notice of him doing so and I'm massively relieved. By now, I'm so cued up that I'd stop *breathing* if that would make them like me more.

He asks them, "Do you need any help? Because if not, I thought I'd show Ly the rest of the house."

"Go ahead, we're fine. Your father won't be home for at least another hour anyway, so why don't you go relax? You already set the table, right?"

Nodding, Colin leads me up the stairs. The extreme

narrowness of the house makes it impossible to have more than two rooms on any floor. On the second, he shows me the "drawing room"—with its long oak dining table, beautifully set for dinner, and a grand piano. Rich paneling and many books. A peek into his father's study—more books—more oak—a comfortable reading corner—then up the stairs, to the third floor.

"The bathroom's there, if you need it. That's my parents' bedroom. And this is my room, from when I still lived here."

We go in. Southern light pours in the large window at the end of the room, spilling over buffed hardwood floors. There's no furniture beyond a bed—he explains that he transplanted most of his things when he moved out, and I look at the items left—a lot of photographs of him, in various dance troupes—some solo shots. I stop in front of one and have the urge to ask him to give it to me. He says:

"My mother set this room up as a shrine as soon as I moved out. I swear I didn't have pictures of myself up when I lived here."

For once, he's the one looking embarrassed, so I change the subject.

"...Thanks for inviting me for dinner. Your family is really great."

"Sorry, what?"

I remember, turn around—his eyes are on my face.

"I just wanted to say thanks, for inviting me to dinner. Your family is so nice."

"Oh." He smiles. "Well, I'm glad you like them— they like you too, but I knew that they would."

"That's good... I... I was kind of freaked out about meeting them. When I asked my roommate how to get here and she saw the address—she psyched me out and I was scared that maybe your parents would be... I don't know..."

"Stuffy?" He laughs now. "Snobby? No, I mean, this house was my uncle's. He was the rich one. He and my aunt never had kids, and my mom's parents died early, so my mom grew up in this house. She was actually an understudy dancer for the Boston Ballet in her twenties—she stopped when she married my father; she got a bad back injury around that time... You'll meet my dad soon—you'll see. Our family's very laid-back. But I have to admit, I was wondering before why you came all dressed up, when I told you on the phone that it's a little get-together. Now I know."

He's teasing me and I redden—

"I'm overdressed."

"No, no." He steps up to me and puts a hand on my shoulder. "You look good."

And I jerk so noticeably that he steps back—

Let me say something here—you know my pathetically short relationship history by now, but just so you don't misunderstand; if I jerk at his touch, it's not because I don't want it—I DO—but as entire chunks of my human instinct, talent and expression seem to have been redirected elsewhere—or even sacrificed at the expense of a certain social competence—I stand there in his room rained in awkwardness, much like the few times we'd sat in his car after dates, when I watched him tapping on the steering wheel, getting euphoric from the tendons of his arms. Trying to figure out if this person could possibly be extending spiritual and friendship-guidance to Ly(sandrze) O'Neil, as a dancer, as an artist—to *me*.

Hard to believe because the boy was an adult—mature—man—who'd toured North America, Europe, Asia—he'd danced in major shows, minor ones, and didn't try to swathe himself in any faux mystery. Colin opened any door I pointed to, and the more he revealed, the more he casually added to his own experience until I realized I had comparatively no experiences and zero glamour whatsoever—

And systematically went numb whenever he tried to touch me.

I couldn't tell if it was pure fright, or an unconsciously foresightful maneuver on my body's part to delay his sexual disappointment and inevitable overall uninterest in me as long as humanly possible. We had few chances to go out (he was always busy) but the last time I sat with him in the car, we kissed long, long, until we were both breathing unbearably heavy—and he asked me if I wanted to go back to his place. Out of all possibly appropriate responses to give right then: of course, yes, please, thank you, nothing more I had wanted to do since I first saw you, let's go, right now, nodding and smiling suffices when words won't come, but I wanted to make him feel so good, wanted to heavypet him all night *so much*; that I jumped out of his car right away, babbling about having to get up early—certain I had raised an expectation (haha) I couldn't meet.

"Alright. Good night, then," he murmured grudgingly, too refined to grope me in the car. He beckoned as an afterthought and I leaned down through the opened window for a reproachfully hot kiss.

"Ly. You're an awful tease."

"I'm sorry."

A meek apology seemed better than telling the truth:

Actually, I'm erotically unfashionable and terrified.

Into kittenish interaction.

And I don't know what you're into nor how to ask.

Which is where we stand now, in his old bedroom, facing each other.

He takes his hand off my shoulder, straightens my collar and grins when I shudder.

"You weren't kidding—you really are nervous." Moves to the desk at the window, takes out a box from one of the drawers, digs deep into it, then throws me a bag. It's got a couple of marijuana buds on the bottom, and a small, separately wrapped, chocolaty tab—he tells me it's hash.

"We won't be eating for another hour at least and I've got a small pipe."

I smile and shake my head.

"Thanks, but... I don't smoke."

Colin puts the bag away while I thumb through his leftover CD collection. Stop on one and put it into his player.

Cake—"Perhaps, Perhaps, Perhaps."

He says, "You don't smoke, you don't drink, you don't eat, you don't screw. A total straight-edge. So, how do you get your kicks?"

I don't answer either, just hit play. I love this song, always have—the Doris Day version in *Strictly Ballroom* is THE version, but in a pinch, this cover isn't bad. The beat rustles the air and I turn my head sharply—raise an eyebrow at him. Under the circumstances, I don't know what else to do, but he responds to it well.

You won't admit you love me, and so?
How am I ever to know?

Colin takes two steps towards me and stretches his hand out to mine. Only one of us can lead, and I know ballroom dance is not his wheelhouse and it's not mine either—but I've always loved the rhumba, and I dance it well, even if I have to be the woman. Colin spins me slowly, until my back is against his stomach—with his hearing, I've been wondering what dancing with him would be like, but his rhythm is sure and perfect. If anything, once we touch, I feel him enter an extra dimension of awareness. Like my body is a litmus he reads and adjusts to instantaneously; anticipating me, moment by moment. We are close to the same height, but he is taller and I have the slighter build. Once I am nestled against him, he takes my left leg, bends it, starting at my upper thigh, runs his fingers to my knee, my calf. Stretches it, my torso lightly wraps around, and I enjoy the feel of the muscles relaxing—releasing—until I have no muscles anymore, no bones, no body—complete fluidity. He cocks his hip to a beat; spins me back. Dips me low. I could swear the top of my head is about to brush the floor, as if my back could touch the backs of my legs.

My arched stomach presses against his concave one, my pelvis grinds into his as I pull myself up, feel the vertebrae stack up, one by one. His fingertips guide the rising motion from my lower back, barely touching me. My fingers slowly slide over his clavicles and come to a rest behind his neck.

And my lips come to a stop.

Before his.

We don't smile.

Then he tilts back and releases himself. For a half-second, we are in free fall, but I don't pull back and we fall on the bed behind him.

We sink—the bed—Colin—I'm on top.

The sheets are very clean.

I stroke him lightly, clumsily open his fly. Feel him push against me, *see, I just needed to dance with you.*

"I should lock the door," is the last thing I say.

"It's fine. Nobody will ever come all the way up here."

Everything happens too fast to worry or think. Next thing I know, I'm off the bed, kneeling over him. I've only done this once or twice in my life before and never to completion. Colin closes his eyes again, which is good, I wouldn't want him to watch. He sounds like he's enjoying it, which is encouraging, then grabs my shoulder—says my name, I know, he's warning me—but I don't take my mouth away. I sit up, slightly shaking, running my fingers over his taut stomach under his shirt and his muscles won't stop twitching under my hands, like the coat of a stallion. He wipes a drop off my mouth with a finger—

"Was that the first time you...?"

"Was it bad?" I turn my face away.

"Of course not. You were just very careful. So I wondered."

"Not the very first time... but..." (The first time I swallowed.) My tongue feels bleached and I whisper into his ear. "Anyway, I forgot to ask you before—but I'm here as a friend, right?"

He sits up and hugs me.

"If that's how you want to be here. But my parents were asking if you're my boyfriend."

"Oh." And I feel exceedingly happy—close, like when we danced the rhumba—like when I sank onto the bench next to him at the park after we had walked around. He pulls me over to him and starts to doze lightly, then falls into deeper sleep and, far from disappointed, I'm glad he's forgotten me—anything else would be improper. Tracing his cheekbone with one finger while he sleeps is the boldest I get. Colin's eyelids tremble, but he doesn't open them, only rubs me over my pants, groggily and without conviction, while I lay next to him, breathing the air he breathes out. Even that is clean. All of him seems pure and I sigh, content in his company. He doesn't regain consciousness, nor stop rubbing me, and I figure I'll come privately, quietly, and clean up in the bathroom before dinner. Inconveniencing him by taking off my clothes or waking him doesn't occur to me.

This is the natural order of things.

Having him please me seems a supreme privilege I shouldn't easily receive.

10

I wouldn't mind becoming closer to my other roommates, but somehow end up only talking to Valerie. Michael (the fledgling banker) and I have absolutely nothing in common. My first impression of him from when he interviewed me over the phone for the room was pretty spot: a bro's bro who adores the Sox. I remember one night I had come home from a late class. He was piled in the living room with his friends, swilling tepid Pabst, eyeing a taped game.

"Yo," Mike called out when he heard me rattling the door. "Come watch the game with us?"

I wanted to go to bed but figured I should at least go into the living room for a few minutes, to say hi. I regretted that decision immediately, because a girl pressed a beer into my hand—another one pushed me onto the couch. I sat wedged between Mike's girlfriend and another girl, drinking lukewarm piss and watching a sport I have minus 100 interest for, but I was still buzzed from work and the beer put a nice fuzz on it, until I felt the girl next to me put her hand on my leg. My thigh flexed from her touch and she playfully drew a nail across my knee.

"You're so tense," she giggled at me.

I've known a few guys who love to lead straight women on, enjoying the moment when they can drop the bomb of their total unavailability, but that was a game I didn't play. Not to mention, girls were as perpetually unattracted to me as I was to them. Was I misreading something? Beer and tiredness swirled in me, and

I wasn't quite sure what to say. Mike's girlfriend Kelsey smiled at her friend. "He probably strained himself dancing. Ly is a dancer. Did you know that?"

"Oh...?" The girl stroked my leg harder now, and I felt like an exotic animal getting poked by a stick—. She leaned into me, huggy and close and I half expected her to start making out with me, but then Kelsey dropped the other shoe, with considerable gusto.

"Don't try so hard, Brianna. He's gay."

The girl took her hand off of me fast as you please and I sipped the Pabst with a slight sadistic smile—

Then there was Mira, our other roommate. I saw her hardly ever. Though she preferred to study behind closed doors, once or twice a week she left her door open, perhaps to air the room out. Walking by, you could get a glimpse of a cell-like space filled almost entirely by a king-sized bed—books piled up on the floor all around. No furniture, no decoration—a single dim bulb pulsing from the ceiling and a sallow girl lying on her stomach in a nest of papers and binders. Highlighting her notes in the dank miasma of unwashed clothes and forgotten take-out boxes. I never felt obliged to do more than wave and walk by.

Which left Valerie.

I ran into her in the kitchen often enough—when I was eating breakfast, or if I was making "dinner," and she would join me sometimes for a little conversation— always nicely suited, always terribly makeuped, though I found myself gradually losing the traces of my first-impression hostility.

Even if our talks were one-sided. Valerie rarely

asked questions. Her curiosity towards me or my work at the studio dipped under zero, but she did not seem to consider the possible mutuality of this emotion. Irritated at first, I became used to hearing long narratives of her life and found out many things about her, starting with her job. Apparently, she was the assistant dean at a local technical school, not too far from our apartment.

"Really?" I shoveled steamed rice onto a plate while I explained that I didn't expect someone so young to have such a high position.

"I'm not that young, Ly," she simpered at me. I raised an eyebrow. She knew my age, but I didn't know hers, only imagined she was somewhere in her late twenties. Then found out I was almost a decade off. Valerie was my first lesson in "people in their thirties can still look like normal people." Though I guess it wasn't a completely wrong assumption on my part: people her age didn't generally live in a hodge-podge flat of strangers renting rooms. But still, she had a nice job, as fitting a nice girl who came from a nice family—originally from upstate New York and, as she had said the first day, a bona fide WASP—"I wanted to be a doctor, but my oldest brother Pete beat me to that—then my second oldest sibling became a lawyer. I didn't want to be accused of being a copycat, so I went into admin."

She told me a lot about her boyfriend too, a guy she frequently compared to young Brad Pitt, in both figure and face. The day when I finally met Robert, she grabbed my arm in the kitchen after he had lumbered off to use the bathroom.

"So, what do you think? Is he a catch or what?"

I concluded (to myself only) that yes, Robert could pass as Brad Pitt, in a dark alley, after someone had consumed at least four shots of tequila.

"He's a good looking guy, sure..." was my vague answer.

Brad came out, and though she made an attempt at us to all have a chummy conversation, we didn't really talk. He struck me as strange, even stranger than Valerie—a sullen, morose type of dude. They seemed incompatible and unaffectionate with each other, but as soon as he left, Valerie got as flighty as ever and told me that they were going to get married soon. She was just waiting for his parents to come around. They lived close to Boston College; Brookline Heights (a name-drop that was lost on me, as she saw by my blank expression, so she explained)—they were Jewish gentry who weren't too happy about their oldest son marrying a Gentile. Nor were her own parents happy about her wanting to marry into a family who didn't think their princess was Good Enough.

"But I'll show them," she said ominously while we sat at the kitchen table. Her face got hard then, and it made me wonder about her. Her face had few expressions, but hardness was one of them, as if she was out to prove something—but I don't know what or to who. Michael beefed with her regularly. As the longest tenant, he was the unofficial head of our apartment and gathered our rent money each month to pass on to the landlord. Sometimes, he complained to me that Valerie would dodge her share, or would ask for an extension, and had once even asked to borrow money from him.

I questioned this again, because when *we* talked, it was about her hyper-rich parents, their winter trips to the Bahamas, her great job—her dollar-decked boyfriend; until I began to believe that these were maybe lies she had concocted to... impress... me?

I rejected that idea when I could find no reason for why she would want to do such a thing. Still, I couldn't deny. Something about her didn't fit. Yet at times her loneliness seemed palpable and I felt a weird and implacable... poignancy? Towards her. And that didn't fit either.

One night, I was walking home from Helena's studio when I passed the college near our apartment where Valerie worked. She had offhandedly mentioned earlier that she would be eating out of the vending machine that night—they were working out a grant, and nobody would be leaving the building until it was done. I passed the Mexican place down the street where I knew she liked the takeout, remembered our conversation in the morning and got her a burrito—then took it to the college.

The security guard's eyeballs sprouted hairs when I asked for Valerie Beaumont's desk—of course. I was in my dance clothes still, burningly out of place in the tech college, and she and I had the uncanny-valley–age-gap that made me too young to be her boyfriend and too old to be her son. The guard was probably wondering who the hell I was.

"Oh yes, she's back there."

Her name was on a tablet by the door (though not her title) and I thought it was a rather insignificant office for an Assistant Dean—but I stepped in and when she saw me, her eyebrows furrowed.

"Oh. Ly. What are you doing here?"

I felt silly all of the sudden, like I had done something we were not close enough for. Guilt washed me. I could mime the nice guy doing an overworked roomie a solid, all I wanted—my real reason for dropping in was to see if her story about working here checked out. And it did. Sort of. So now what?

"I don't know. I remembered what you said earlier, about not having dinner tonight, and I passed by Tacho's and thought of you."

I put the burrito on her desk and her reaction was so odd, I stepped back. She started to *cry*.

"No one's ever done something so nice to me before," she whispered, and I nodded, swallowed and ran away. Like a kid who had left a flaming cat turd on someone's porch.

I felt like I had played a nasty trick on her.

That same night it is bitterly cold. I was complaining to Colin recently because the insulation in our apartment is ridiculously bad—and the very concept of "insulation" was not something I had ever had to ponder, growing up in Southern California.

"Those old building are all like that. You should put plastic wrap on the inside of your window—it's what I did when I was living in an old brownstone," he suggested, which seemed like an absurd course of action, but lying in bed that night, shivering under my comforter in long johns and a thermal shirt, I'm ready to consider embracing the absurd the very next day. The dark in my room is a pulsey, shadowy blue. Ominous, but made more cheery by the sound of a few drunks celebrating outside.

Then comes the knock on my door.

Short and soft. Like a timid ghost.

Initial reaction: *Who the hell?*

"Who is it?" I ask and focus my bleary eyes on the clock next to my bed. The digital numbers show that I've been tossing and turning for over four hours. It's just before three in the morning and I'm frozen and exhausted. The door swings open—I wonder which one of my roommates needs something at this ungodly hour. Maybe Michael is drunk and has confused my room with his? But no, it's Valerie. She stands in my door, wearing nothing but a thin long T-shirt and a thong.

"Ly."

That's my name, don't wear it out.

"...Yes?"

"It's freezing in my room."

I don't know why I feel so irritated, as she has not woken me up, and I almost snap, *What the hell do you want me to do about it?*, but hold it back.

"Valerie. It's... in the middle of the night."

She looks sheepish then. "I'm sorry, I couldn't sleep. Did I wake you up?"

I can't lie.

"No... but... what are you doing here?"

In the dark, it's hard to see her face, but I can tell she has it turned down towards her feet. "I'm really cold."

"Maybe it's because you're trying to sleep half naked."

"I always sleep like this." She shrugs her shoulders. "Anyway—you know how bad the insulation is. You and I have the outside rooms. We've got the bad deal. I feel like I could wear a parka to bed and still freeze."

"Why don't you try wearing a parka anyway?"

I lie back down, and she walks over to me.

"I was hoping that maybe I could sleep in your bed? It would be warmer..."

I sit back up sharply, sure she's kidding, but she's not. Now I remember that day when she interrupted my shower. Her face was amused then, as if enjoying my shock, but there is no cocky bravura about her now. She makes herself small—and I get an intense ball in the pit of my stomach—not revulsion, something more like fear, but not quite; another emotion for her and it's NOT desire—because even if I was attracted to a woman, she would be negative my type. Still, I can't put my finger on it. The whole situation is bizarre. Maybe I'm still asleep.

"Valerie, are you for real?"

"Come on, Ly. We both have someone and you know how I feel about Robert—and I know how you feel about women. This isn't like that. I really am freezing my butt off. You want me to knock on Mira's door and ask her? I'll do it. Up in New York, my sister and I used to sleep in one bed together all the time."

"I'm not your sister."

She shivers then, and I get an image of a kitten, stranded, on a bank of snow.

...

"Goddammit." I roughly turn the cover away and let her get into bed. She gets in close to the wall, and I pull the covers over us.

"Don't touch me though," I growl—and she shrinks back against the wall—while I wonder why I'm getting so gruff with her. Maybe it's that I'm scared, because I've never been in bed with someone without romantic intent. Or in bed with anyone really, for sleep. I had yet to spend a full night with Colin, and hadn't ever with anyone back home.

Now I stretch out my body, feeling more awake than ever. The presence of another person really does make it warmer quickly though. I can feel her heating up the sheets from her side, making the bed nice and toasty under the covers. She falls asleep or pretends to, at least, and then pulls closer to me.

I don't do anything to stop her.

She puts her arms around me.

I let her.

Valerie moulds her body to me, and I want to say something, but somehow feel like it still isn't enough, so I wait for her to do something objectionable, something undeniably transgressive, so that I can get good and pissed and kick her out—but after that, she doesn't move. I realize she really is asleep. And my vicious doubt cools while I fall asleep too, chilled by guilt. Maybe sometimes, people really are just cold.

Or lonely.

"You know I love you, but what the hell are you doing?"

We were standing in F____ Hall, place stuffed to chaos with the post-Halloween shoppers, in the thronged food area, waiting to get to the front of the seafood line. A little girl standing with her mom at the Chinese joint next to us was staring at me, so I did a silly little dance. That made her laugh—and she pulled on her mom's sleeve, to get the woman's attention, but as soon as her mother turned, I stood stock still, facing forward, more serious than a guard at Buckingham. The mother scolded the little girl for staring and turned away again. The kid looked back at me helplessly—Colin was directly in front of me in line, and I stepped back slightly and raised my left leg—the knee bent—higher, until I stretched it (this is only possible in these really old soft skinny jeans) and rested my ankle gently on Colin's shoulder in a vertical split, my arms wrapped around him, my head against his neck. Eyes closed in bliss.

This move is the color of total love.

"Mommy, look!" she whined, and the woman turned just as my leg was already lowered, my hands in my pockets. I whistled.

The little girl stuck her tongue out at me. A woman next to us started laughing. Colin turned around.

"Seriously, was that your freaking *shoe* on my new jacket? What are you doing?"

"Relax, I barely touched you. I'm messing with that kid over there."

"And everyone else in line." He took our food: lobster bisque in a bread bowl—a glass of sparkling water for me. We looked for a spot to sit in the cavernous dining hall area, with the snippets of a hundred conversations bouncing around us.

"Eat," Colin ordered me. "Don't give me that 'my stomach can't take it' horsecrap."

I dipped a small chunk of sourdough into the soup, but my stomach had been better lately—we'd been walking around all afternoon shopping and were both craving something hot after the chill outside. Boston hadn't seen snow yet, but the days lately felt bitterly cold. It was the start of my first East Coast winter: beautiful and trying to kill me.

"So." Colin wiped his mouth. "When can I tell Marichka that you're coming in for an audition? What's that face? Someone has to remind you."

"Maybe next year."

"Perfect, because there will be audition slots for late next January, for spring term. Did you download and finish your application?"

"Yes."

"...Did you *send* your application?"

I gulped.

"No."

"Alright. Are you fucking joking me? The deadline is at the end of next week."

Colin didn't usually swear. It was a warning shot and my eyes went all around the hall.

"And if I miss it, that's not on you, but me," I said, my tone as rude as I dared.

If we were brothers, this is where he would've decked me. He looked like he wanted to anyway.

"Stop being a punk," he rumbled. "And send in your application tomorrow. Or I will be very pissed. I already told Marichka all about you—I got her excited to see you dance, so do *not* ruin this over a technicality. You cannot audition for her if you don't apply to the school proper."

"Sure, great, put more pressure on me."

When Colin got mad (and it was not often), he didn't raise his voice; he *lowered* it, which made it so much worse. It sounded like benzene getting poured out on concrete—right before someone strikes a match and torches it all to fire.

"You don't want me to put pressure on you. You can't handle pressure? Then quit dancing, Ly—because from here on out, *it will be nothing but pressure.* And if you've been in this since you could walk, you know that. You are wasting away in that studio and you don't have to. Right now, you can still get back. It will be hard, but you can do it. Wait another six months, and you really will be teaching kids for the rest of your life. If you can't handle pressure, then go ahead and do that. But I know you. You have to be on stage. I mean, look at you." He sneered then, the tiniest sneer. "You're a total attention whore."

I rolled my eyes. "No, I'm not."

He touched my hair (bleached, dyed blue), my jacket (held together by tape, zippered, the faded red of dried ketchup), my ears (three holes on the right side, two on the left, all different studs, all home-punched, courtesy of my crazy best friend back home, Trischa).

"Ly, you can't be in a public place for five minutes without getting someone to look at you. You put yourself out there. You're a performer. Just accept it."

I kept my mouth shut, remembering my ma:

Lysandrze, please change, you canNOT wear that outside!

My brother, when we were still younger:

Stop that, everyone is staring! Stop showing off.

Show-off, show-off, and they never understood what Colin does, because he's a dancer too: we *need* to show off. We need people to look at us and admire us and want us constantly, or we shrivel up *and die*—nowhere was I ever more at home than on stage with every eye in the auditorium petting my body, so why was I putting it off—? And unspoken but another thing drilled into me since kidhood. I could be an amazing dancer all I wanted: talent and hard work *aren't enough*. Plenty have both—you also need that stroke of luck. Colin was my good luck charm: offering that foot in the door all talents about to sink into obscurity dream of. I had to stop being insane about this.

After finishing the soup, we walked out—Colin spent twenty minutes lazily hunting around for potential Christmas presents. Told me it takes him for EVER to find the right things, so he likes to start early. He ended up buying something for his older sister. We cut through the Common, then got to his car. The sun kept sinking—the cold shivery disk ducked out of sight while we passed by the Charles, and the water looked blacker than onyx.

"So how much money would someone have to pay

you before you agreed to take a polar bear swim? That water must be hella cold." I pressed my nose to the window but Colin shook his head.

"You're not used to it, but this is nothing yet. Come out here right after Christmas or sometime in January with me—it's frozen solid. You can walk out on it."

"Really?"

"Yeah. You know, I've always had this crazy dream to do a dance on the frozen Charles. Something contemporary—when there's a layer of snow, so there's still some traction—something beautiful."

"Well, why not? We'll come out here during January and do that dance."

He drove me home, and I got ready to jump out while the engine was still running, but there was an empty parking spot right in front of our building. It seemed like an omen.

"Do you want to park the car and come up?"

"There's a game on tonight I wanted to catch."

I shook my head and clicked my tongue.

"I forgot, you like that."

"Yes. I like football and I like *West Side Story*. 'Well-rounded' is the term. Anyway, if you want to hang out more, I can watch at your place—would any of your roommates be watching?"

"Michael will be, I bet."

But Michael wasn't home. We left our shoes in the hall, stepped into the living room. I asked him what he wanted to drink without thinking about the fact that I've got nothing but herbal tea, but then realized there were a few bottles of wine abandoned by various houseguests and proclaimed as up for grabs. He looked them over and picked a white. We settled on the couch and I got bored enough to drink. After one and a half glasses, my interest for the game had risen significantly—"What are they doing that for? What is that sign?" I kept asking, but he stopped explaining after a while, claiming that I was a lost cause. Maybe he was right. I stared at the screen, crying of boredom, then tried to distract him— he shook his head—"Stop it." Finally, I had his attention, and we were making out heavy when the front door opened. We didn't separate and I heard Valerie's voice.

"Now here's a sight for sore eyes."

I unlocked myself from his neck and looked up at her, beaming.

"Oh, hey Valerie. This is my boyfriend. Colin."

Her smile was vinegary.

"The infamous Colin Alexander Savoy. I've been seeing your name in the margins of our newspapers for weeks. Let me guess. You're a dancer too."

I was too tipsy to be embarrassed by her, but Colin motioned towards the wine bottle without answering. I wondered if he maybe hadn't heard what she'd said.

"Care to join us? I can get another glass."

"No, thanks. I actually just came from a drink with my boyfriend, so I'm going right off to bed. But you boys have fun."

She left the room and an hour or so later so did we. Colin took the glasses into the kitchen. I went back to my room. A few minutes later, he came back too, bringing a bowl. He put it in my hands.

"It's fat-free plain yogurt. And some dried fruit. I guessed that it's yours? Eat it."

The fruit was not mine but probably Mira's. She seemed to eat a lot of desiccated things. Me, I don't eat fruit. I don't eat Red Things. I looked down: the shriveled nuggets were reanimated by the yogurt wet. Berry blood smeared into the white, in melting beads. Come. Offal. Radioactive pink puddle the kid next to me had horked onto the floor in fourth grade. All of those dissolved into the bowl I was holding, and I could smell butyric acid. No, I won't be eating this. Why didn't Colin know that? Because I hadn't told him: Classic *Whatever you do, don't be yourself.* I tried to shelter him from my food issue as much as possible and let him interpret it as a run of the mill eating disorder. That's what I wanted to be to him: commonly, not uncommonly strange. So I avoided the yogurt's eyes and began spooning it into my body. Colin looked happy.

"That's good, Ly. I worry about you. Are you taking those vitamins I brought last time?"

"I take like. Two thousand RDA of. Everything. Every day."

Crisis averted: he laughed. "OK, good. I don't want you getting scurvy or dropsy."

"Or gout," I added. "Don't forget the gout."

"You get gout from overeating. But anyway, it's late and the forecast said it might freeze tonight... I should really get going."

"You could just stay over," I offered. He never had before. "You should know though." An amendment. "That this room gets colder than Satan's butthole."

"Oh, is Satan's anus the ultimate in cold?"

"The North Pole is Bali compared to that."

We went and brushed our teeth, then got back to my room, and he slipped off his clothes and got under the covers. I kicked off my jeans too, kept on my shirt, and he turned off the light next to the bed once I crawled in. We started kissing; slowly—I kept my hands on him, running them over his body, seeing its detail with my fingertips. Too drunk to be disconcerted, I touched his peerlessness until my consciousness demolished into a single locomotive thought. *Damn, you are fine, I want you, I want you, I want you...*

Then I heard him chuckling.

"What?" I asked, afraid.

We still hadn't been together enough times for me to have any confidence and I ran my tongue over my teeth. Were they mossy? No, I'd just brushed them. Paranoid, I adjusted my hands. Anything from my sheets to my technique seemed subject to criticism. But he didn't criticize.

"Nothing, I suddenly remembered. How you said your roommate was a weirdo. Back when I first brought you home."

"Oh, you mean Valerie?"

"Yeah. You were totally right. I saw exactly what you meant, back there in the living room."

"But you... barely talked to her at all."

"I don't mean what she *said*. My eyes were on the TV when she came in, so I didn't really catch it. I meant her manner in general. But... you... do know why she's like that, right?"

He smiled again and I could imagine his mouth clearly in the dark. Well but not overly defined edges, with the corners curled in a perpetual smirk—full, girl-pink—and with the recent cold, faintly chapped. I melted into him.

"No?"

"And here's why I like you, Ly. Sometimes, you're so naïve, it breaks me up. That girl is acting weird because she wants you *so fucking bad*, she doesn't know what to do with herself."

"That's not the reason." I tensed all over and he murmured into my neck.

"You're terrible at reading people and I won't argue with you."

"No, it really isn't."

Because she's slept in my bed before and didn't try anything.

Is what I did NOT say, thank god I wasn't that drunk, but Colin wasn't listening to me anymore. He'd passed a point—and so had I. The wine had loosened me up. I didn't feel the normal anxiety, and let him do whatever he wanted, and it felt good, but then his fingers slid up the backs of my thighs and my entire body clenched.

"Sorry." He stopped his hand immediately and whispered into my ear. "You don't... like that?"

"I... guess not." I was blood-red and too embarrassed to tell him that I hadn't tried it, but the idea had never appealed. Neither to have it done to me, nor to do it to someone else.

"It's not a big deal," he told me, sensing my quiet. "Some guys just don't."

Still, I felt like I was denying him something. I put

my mouth over him in apology, until he was about to, but I didn't swallow it. I licked it off instead, drop by drop, while he petted my hair, then I fell asleep with my head on his wet stomach, his hand on my face—thinking. If I could purr, I would.

12

Valerie continues to sporadically sleep in my bed. Each time, it is the same. She comes in the dead of night, sometime between one o'clock and three. In the morning when I wake up, she's gone—and I know she wakes up before either Michael or Mira, but each morning after she's come, my first thought on opening my eyes is panic that they've seen her. My fears are absurd. For one, I rarely see either of them anyway—but I worry— what would I say to them if they noticed her leaving my room, or if they asked about it?

"Oh, it isn't what it looks like. It's not like that."

Leaving both them and me to wonder, what exactly *is* it like then?

I've reached the point where I feel a twinge of guilt whenever I see Colin. A smaller, but still palpable one, when I (more rarely) see Valerie's boyfriend, Robert.

Still, whenever she knocks and lets herself in, I don't have the heart to tell her to go. I don't know what I feel for her: if it's pity, or if I'm flattered by the thought of her crushing on me? Perhaps what Colin said is true? It seems highly unlikely. The kind of dudes she likes eat guys like me for breakfast, but even if it was, that would hardly flatter me. Aesthetically and physically, I could not be less interested in her.

But we have a routine. Each time she gets in my bed, she first puts herself close to the wall, almost up against it. As the minutes pass, she incrementally comes closer to me, ending with her arms around my body. I feel her breasts press against my shoulder blades, and the warm triangle where her thighs meet presses into my butt. Sometimes, I sleep more soundly for this presence of her; other times, I lay awake and try to pinpoint what I'm feeling as she puts her body against mine. I conclude that it's not pleasure. I have no desire whatsoever to touch her or even turn around. Yet something about it must appeal to me, because I don't lock my door—I don't confront her in the morning—I don't tell her to get up and leave.

I don't do anything to stop it.

Nor do I tell Colin.

Is this cheating? I ask myself one morning while I'm eating breakfast. I don't *think* so. I figure it can't be cheating, if you have no sexual urge or attraction towards the other person. But my reluctance to tell Colin destroys that rationale. It may not be cheating, but I imagine something about it isn't kosher. I don't want to picture what his face would look like, were I to ever tell him that I allow such a thing to happen on a regular basis. I can see his expression: it would be complete bewilderment. And then Colin has his pride. It's not an empty stereotype, about dancers being vain. Even if he didn't say it, he would be thinking it: You let me and then her of all people get into bed with you? A withering reaction.

I don't say anything to Valerie either. Nothing she does during the day gives the slightest acknowledgment that she sometimes spends the night in my room, which is a relief, as it avoids any awkward tensions with the other roommates, but then it starts to confuse *me*. One day, I run into her in the kitchen after she left my room early that morning, and she says "Good morning" to me, as brightly and as blankly as she would say it to Michael or Mira or the guy selling her daily coffee. I feel bizarrely hurt, as if she is rejecting me on some level, and I grumble a "morning" back while I toast some bread and wonder if I'm being a complete fool.

So I decide to talk to Colin, indirectly. The chance comes up one night at dinner. We're near Harvard Square in the B____ Café—I've just picked through a plate of catfish tacos and he's sipping on a Corona while I tell him about a performance I'm going to give with Helena from the studio. She has asked me to perform at a charity event with a troupe made up of her old dancing colleagues. The group came together a few nights ago to discuss logistics, and once they started drinking, the stories you hear! I'm giving Colin the juicer bits, with names edited out to protect the innocent. Then he's telling me about a guy, a friend of his I've met once or twice, who somehow ended up sleeping with a girl last weekend and has now tailspinned into an identity crisis. We're laughing and joke-cracking, but also sympathetic, and I realize that this might just be the perfect opportunity to ask him.

"So, have *you* ever wanted to sleep with a girl?"

He takes a sip of his drink. "Like, have I fantasized about it?"

"Sure..."

"I suppose? It's not like I've never been attracted to a woman, but if I am, I find that it's just so much—more vague, you know? The attraction I feel to her, or the connection. Than to a man. And that I have no desire to pursue it."

Yeah, I think to myself. That's a good word for it.

Vague.

No desire to pursue it.

"Then you've never slept with a woman?" I go on.

"Do you mean slept with—or sex?"

I turn red. "I guess... sex."

Colin watches the word off my lips.

Looks deep into me.

"Once."

"Because you wanted to see what it was like?"

"No. It wasn't supposed to happen. The girl was from back when I was a student. We were on a show together and then there was this party, thrown at her place—we got into a shot-slamming contest. Never a good idea. She had this thing for me, even though she knew... The next morning, I woke up naked, she's naked next to me, we were too wasted to use a condom, so we both freaked out. Luckily, nothing happened."

I want to ask something sophomoric like, but was it *good?*

Colin reads me like a magazine.

"If you're wondering if I enjoyed it, I don't remember what it was like, at all. It really screwed our friendship though, so I wish it hadn't happened. She was a good friend, but things got tense between us after that. Because she had a crush on me, she kept saying I needed to *explore* if I may be bi, or to come clean and say I was only calling myself gay to get out of dating her. She was convinced I must do one or the other, because 'if you were born gay, you wouldn't have slept with me' is how she put it."

"What about the eight shots of vodka... or whatever you drank?"

"That's what I tried to tell her."

I fleetingly think back to guys I knew back home, like three-week–fling Mitchell; the guys I knew who went out with or had sex with girls, desperately needing to talk themselves into liking it. I personally had never even been on a date with a girl, and I'd thought this whole time that I had an answer to the infamous question. But the answer I was always so sure of had developed a subtle and interesting cataract of late. I ask Colin—

"So I guess you don't consider yourself bi?"

He looks exasperated.

"Would *you*, if you've only had sex with a woman once in your life, and didn't remember it?"

"I guess not."

"Look, like I said, it's not like I'd never thought of a woman in a sexual way—and I think few people are 100 percent a single orientation anyway. But the way I explained it to this girl space friend: if you *need* alcohol to do it, that's a sign you're having sex with the wrong gender."

I lean back, thinking, he's right. Now I can finally let this go. Sleeping in one bed with Valerie means nothing, because even *trying* to picture sex with her, sloshed or otherwise, is impossible. A sleek dancer girl, with a chest flat as a slab; long-leg, boy-face and pure muscle?—Sure, I could faintly see it, but fertile-looking, dumpy, C-cup Valerie? No, no, no, never. Even without the mental imagine, just thinking about it gives me a *negative* erection.

"Why do you ask though," Colin teases me. Brings me back to Earth. "You think you might be bi?"

"Not even close."

But he eggs me on. "You can tell me if you're curious. You want to fuck some girl? See what it's like?"

His crudeness is sharp and unlike him—

I draw back and shake my head.

"No, of course not."

"Good." He smiles and puts his hand on my face almost possessively, jellies my insides, and I don't ask him what we're supposed to be to each other. *I* don't want to see anyone else (which is why Valerie's nocturnal visits are hard to justify), but I still don't hope to have an exclusive hold on Colin. He's gone a lot on the weekends— here, there, auditions, overnight trips, and I'm not delusional, though he called me his boyfriend that day in his old room. Though I consider him my boyfriend.

But the awe I watched him with when he first stepped into Helena's studio to pick up my student Taylor hasn't diminished since we've started seeing each other; nor my shyness towards him in bed. It's the kind of awe that makes it hard for me to understand what he's even doing with me.

13

And later, I will only wonder more and more.

Because him, her; day, night—*you got that right.*

Valerie and I go out and do something together *once.*

Even that is a fluke. I come into the kitchen one morning and she's sitting at the breakfast table, scowling like a displeased dictator. I chance a small "morning," thinking I'll grab some tea and get out of her face double-quick, when she takes out an envelope and literally flings it at me. Of course, because it's paper, instead of the dramatic effect of it sailing across the kitchen and crumpling to ruin against me in slow motion, the missile impotently flutters and lands on the floor, closer to her than myself. When I look at her with the appropriate confusion merited by such a gesture, she asks:

"Do you want to go see a ballet? It's short notice, I'm sorry. It's tonight." She tries to put on a strand of pearls and I walk over, to pick the envelope up.

"I didn't know you like the ballet."

"I *don't,*" she growls. "Robert got me tickets for my birthday tonight because I'm a girl and girls like ballet, right? But then, he sends me a *text* last night, telling me that he'll have to visit with an important client today, and there's no way he'll be back here on time to pick me up. So he tells me to go with a friend tonight and he'll take me somewhere else on a different day. You know, the regular Robert male excuse *shit.*"

It's the first time I've heard this kind of outpouring against the perfectly symmetrical and wonderful Robert, and I stand to the side, letting her get to the end of her rope and back. She says:

"Well, I don't know anyone but you who would honestly enjoy going, and I am NOT going to watch anorexics jump around in tights alone, on my birthday—so just take the tickets and go with your boyfriend or something. You do like ballet, right?"

"Of course," I murmur. Opening the envelope, I see that the demon-lord didn't scrooge on seats. These are floor level, front and dead middle. I whistle. "These are some damn fantastic seats, Valerie—to a great show. ...You really don't want to go?"

"I told you, I don't have anyone to go with."

"I'd go with you."

"I'm sure you'd have more fun going with someone else."

Oh, I'm sure I would too. I think of a long, romantic stroll through town with the smoke-eyed beauty. Just the two of us, then watching the show, then dissecting it, all the way back to his place—and then—. Still, don't I have to try?

"Come on, it's your birthday. You're bringing the tickets, so I'll buy dinner. Unless you'd rather go get a drink with some girlfriends tonight?" The selfish side of me hopes she hates ballet enough to take this route, but—

"No, let's go. If you don't mind going with me, I wouldn't mind seeing a ballet with someone who really enjoys it." She gives me a smile, which right now is really more like a not-grimace, and flings the necklace down on the table with frustration. I silently step over and reach out my hand and she puts the strand into it, letting me clasp it behind her neck. The way her mouth is set makes me wonder again if I've done something I shouldn't have.

I walk into the Central Square P_____ café almost ten hours later. There had been another slight agony in front of my closet, and for a second, I'd thought of wearing the outfit I'd worn to Colin's parents' house that Sunday (Valerie had seemed to like it), but not wanting to send her the wrong message that I was dressing to please her, I vacillated. Nothing "date" and nothing too wild. So I settled on a good pair of black jeans, loose white shirt—(not red) jacket—Converse—my hair set well, but nothing crazy. I had even just toned it the other week, so for once, it wasn't lime or powder blue. The mirror confirmed, I looked groomed but unprovocative, and I headed out for our meeting spot.

Valerie's sitting at a front table, reading *The Globe* and sipping a venti what-the-fskjdfs when I walk in. She takes one look, screws her screw-colored myopic eyes on me and pronounces:

"You look gay."

My eyeballs roll back.

"I *am* gay." Someone at the next table seems amused by our exchange and starts to laugh. I laugh too. "Here, I have an idea. If you don't like my clothes, why don't you call Robert and ask him if he can lend me some, oh I don't know, pressed CHINOS with darts, gotta have the darts, and some *performance moccasins*, and a Tommy Hilfiger windbreaker."

"It's not the clothes," she huffs. "I don't want to go out with a guy wearing more jewelry than me."

"I'm not wearing jewelry!" I snap and she jumps up and grabs my ears, tutting loudly. (Whoops, took out the lip ring but forgot the studs.)

I think blackly: *And AYE don't want to go out with a middle-aged kindergarten-teacher–dressing hetero binch with a stick up her___!!!* But I don't say it. I won't wound her feelings on her birthday. It's true though: she's wearing some kind of wine-colored pantsuit (???) and her hair is pulled back with a banana clip (!). I snicker and think of that show my ma and I used to watch. *Sex and the City.* You were right, Carrie—scrunchies (and, I would argue, banana clips), belong on ten-year-old girls in the nineties or those sweaty babes in the *Call On Me* video. But not on real women in a decent-sized metropolitan city. There's just no excuse.

With my inner bitch revved, the night goes down from here. Valerie wants to go to an Italian place on Newberry Street. The menu is an orgy of eggs, butter, cream, cheese, pancetta, bruschetta, frittatas, potattas, garlic, tomatoes, and all kinds of things that wreak havoc on my stomach. Gleefully overpriced too. Why the hell did I offer to pay? I pick at a melancholic side salad while she twirls spaghetti carbonara onto her fork and complains.

"Eating with you makes me feel like a pig."

I shrug. That's not my fault, right? But she can't stop sniping.

"So what is this, anyway? A food allergy? I can't wait for this food-allergy *fashion* to finally be over. Everybody has at least two." She mimics a prissed voice. "'Oh, I'm allergic to gluten; I'm allergic to black pepper; I'm allergic to parsley!' Just when I thought vegans were getting really annoying, all the whiny food allergists started coming out of the woodwork."

As my fashion- and social media crazed friend from home Trischa would say: Don't feed the troll. Identify it—then ignore it. And I want to, but I can't resist aiming low.

"I dunno. Feels like there's a much higher chance of running into a whiny trust-fund baby in Boston, than a vegan."

From our conversations in the apartment, I've determined: the thing she seems to hate most about having money is not being able to crow about bootstraps. Valerie looks like she wants to belt me.

"That's not fair. I told you already that my parents wouldn't support me after college. I've worked for every penny I have now."

I don't mention that, while that's true, she didn't have to start a couple ten in the hole because they didn't make her work for the money she didn't have back when she got the sleek college education that got her the sleek job. Still, I put my head down, conceding, and she picks the ball up from further back.

"You don't want to tell me what you're allergic to?"

Like I'll get into that convo: I'm allergic to food looking GROSS. To foods touching each other. To nasty aesthetic. I glower over the roll basket. "It's not an allergy. My stomach is just tweaked. It always has been."

"So why don't you go to the doctor? You're horribly underweight. It looks terrible."

"So sorry Madame doesn't like my looks. But I'm not underweight. Not for a dancer. And I have gone to plenty of doctors—I've been going since I was a little kid. I mean, I don't anymore, because there's no point. They haven't come up with any reason."

"You're trying to tell me that NO doctor has been able to give you a decent diagnosis or a clue as to what is wrong with your digestion?"

I blow her a kiss over the table.

"One did, once. He told me I shouldn't play with myself so much."

Valerie lasers me. "No wonder you don't know what's wrong with you. You don't take it seriously."

My shrug is dismissive, but I wonder if my stomach's twitchiness tonight isn't because of her. After that exchange, we don't talk—in fact, what has always been clear becomes even more so. We have no common ground, and I find myself cruelly wishing that I had just taken the other ticket when she'd offered and asked Colin. We'd be having a blast now. Then I feel bad, figuring that she's probably still pissed at Robert, so I try to get her to talk about her day. All that does is uncork a real genie of a rant regarding the incompetent goons she has to kissass to. Each minute of pretending to listen makes me die a little more inside.

We finally make it to the concert hall—check our coats—get our programs—and the shittiness of the night thus far gets washed away by the pre-show excitement and glow. I'm almost jumping out of my seat, because I haven't been to a ballet yet here in Boston and I *love* Romeo and Juliet, in all its manifestations: the play, the movie by Baz Luhrmann, and of course, the ballet. And this place is so lovely, and the set pieces are so flawless—and—and—

"You're like a... puppy about to piss itself. Can't you settle down?" Valerie looks over at me squirming, but I can't help but beam at her.

"Thanks for inviting me. Really. This is so perfect."

Without thinking, I reach over and squeeze her hand.

By 'this,' I mean the stage, the seats, the setting, the mood, the opera house, the dancing that is yet to come, but she blushes. Tentatively squeezes my hand back. I let out a squeak; the music starts, and my unease floats away with the rise of the first note from the orchestra's pit. If I had to pick one word for how the performance that night made me feel, it would be 'entranced.' I look over as the Montagues and Capulets start leaping and brawling on stage, so that I can gush *sotto voce* with Valerie about how great this is—and I see with disappointment that her eyes are already closed. By the time the lovers pour their souls out to each other via dance, her mouth is flopped open.

She drinks champagne during intermission (which helps her sleep even better during the second half), and at the end of the show, I have no one to exchange impressions, opinions and critique with because she never saw past "Do you bite your thumb at us, sir?".

I conclude as we sit silently in the taxi barreling us home that as people, as friends, our connection is flatter than a week-opened can of three dead flies in it Coke. Once we're back in the apartment, I shower, brush my teeth and, on the way to bed, I see Valerie sitting in the kitchen in a robe, reading something. No more pit of bitterness and entitlement and spite; just a small and rumpled ball, and though I'm still pissed at how thoroughly *un-fun* she managed to render a potentially great night, I have my first stab of doubt. Is there something I could've done? Should I have tried harder? She looks up and I suddenly remember what has been missing from the day. The Birthday Song. So I smile, walk forward, strike a pose in the kitchen's doorframe and, channeling my inner Marilyn, sing her the breathiest, sexiest, silliest "Happy Birthday, Mr. President" I can muster—at one point, she can't take it anymore and starts cracking up and I finish the song and sink into the splits in front of her.

"It's your birthday for twenty more minutes, but after this night, you're probably wishing you did just call one of your friends for a drink, instead of hanging out with a bitchy twink."

But she smiles genuinely for once.

"Ly, when Robert told me that he wouldn't be able to make it, I more or less convinced myself that I would not have fun today no matter what. I wanted to have a horrible birthday, hate the male race, and wallow in self-pity. I should be the one apologizing for ruining your night, but I did enjoy myself with you, and I appreciate you spending time with me and being so patient."

...

I was thinking she might offer me some kind of apology, but after this unexpectedly mushy gush, she looks as dippy as Juliette, and I stare at her thinking,

Huh? You have got to be kidding me.

14

That Thursday, Colin and I have a date, but end the night in our own separate apartments. I have three classes to teach the next day and need a full night of sleep, and Colin has a grueling rehearsal lined up. Also, I will be performing "The Arabian Dance" from *The Nutcracker* for my beginning ballet class at the end of the week and I need to work out some parts. We'll have only two more sessions before the studio closes for winter break. Thinking about it, I'm wandering in that hazy no-man's-land between consciousness and sleep, hearing the smoky reed of the Arabian suite's oboe thread in and out of my ear, when my door opens quietly. Valerie comes in.

I don't sit up anymore. I don't say anything anymore, only scoot over, and she moves behind me and puts herself close to the wall. Today, it's especially cold. I put the plastic wrap on the windows as advised, but with tonight's ripping wind, I can almost feel the gusts come through the window panes.

"I'm frozen," she whispers to me. For once, she talks. Normally, once she's asked me if she can get into bed, we say nothing else.

"Then get closer," I say back, turned away from her like always. I'm still seeing the Arabian Dance in my head, but she dissipates the delicate steps.

"You don't mind? If I touch you?"

"Valerie, you're going to touch me once you fall asleep anyway."

So she worms forward and it's true, her body is icy. I shiver from her touch. I can tell she's wearing what she always does—a long T-shirt, with underwear under-neath—and her thighs are prickled with cold.

"I know what I'm getting you for Christmas. A pair of thick flannel pajamas," I mutter and she wraps her arms around me.

"You sound so grumpy."

"Because I have a long day tomorrow and you're keeping me up."

"I'm sorry."

I cut off the conversation by starting to sleep. Or trying to sleep, because something is different tonight. I remember how the first few times she slept in my bed, I waited almost breathlessly for her to cross a line, and she never did—making me drop the idea that she had suspicious designs, but tonight, her hands don't settle into their normal spots. They seem restless; they move around me, but nowhere definitive. I draw in my breath—I need to tell her to stop, to go to sleep, or to get out, but something about the anonymity of it—she says nothing—the movements are almost purposeless, not sexual, and when I ask myself: "Do you want to touch her?" the answer, honestly, is no. But when I ask myself: "Do you want her to stop touching you?" *that answer is also no.* I keep quiet, but I can't pretend that she's asleep, nor that I am. Once, she brushes against my ribs and I let out the tiniest moan—I've always been very sensitive there and her hearing the sound seems to breaks the spell. Her motion stops, as if I had ordered her to, the hand settles on my waist. I hear her breathing steady—deepen, and I wonder: Should I say something? In the end, she falls asleep.

But I can't.

15

The Arabian Dance ended. I gave Kayley a wink before I did a final back walkover that sank into a full split. My nose rested on my left knee. My body was stretched and at peace. I enjoyed the glow of the finish, of feeling my body slacken, music dying, dead, kids beginning to clap, clapping louder, and then I slowly rose up. Helena gave me a hug, and the kids and I did a last group huddle before they left for two weeks. We still had a class scheduled for our most advanced students, but the younger ones would all take a full break and the studio was unofficially closed now. While the kids were getting changed in the locker room, I talked to Helena, then walked over to Colin. He was actually free that day and had come to pick up Taylor. Now he stood like the sultan and took my hand. I laughed and did a pirouette. He dipped me, then dragged me across the floor in an arabesque—we did an impromptu *pas-de-deux*—Helena watched—then the kids came back in—I quickly threw on a thermal shirt over my "Terrors" tee and we drove Taylor home.

Later that evening, we met again for dinner, dressed to the teeth. The plan was to go swing dancing that night at the CrystalBall, with two dancer friends of his, and there are few things more joyous in this world than putting on a sharp suit I cannot afford (to be dry-cleaned and returned to Filene's for a full refund next week) and dancing swing to a live band with a girl who really knows how to move. My date for the night was a girl called Madi. She had a silky red dress covered in white polka dots and lips redder than a fire-truck. Body lighter than ash. Once we got on the floor, I could throw her and toss her and we did the Jitterbug, the Black Bottom—the Hustle, the Mambo—we did Danny Zuko and Rizzo from *Grease*, the craziest Jive we could dance, until her makeup ran from sweat and she excused herself, laughing, to escape with her friend to the bathroom. Colin was sitting at the bar, drinking a gin tonic. I slipped over to him and ordered just a tonic.

"Good-looking suit." He arched one of his narrow brows at me, and I wanted to, but didn't kiss him. We were playing it straight that night. "You should do that dance for Marichka."

"The Mambo? Sure. I'll see if I can rent Mads out for the audition day."

"Not the Mambo. The Arabian Dance."

"Oh, that one. What... *en travesti?*"

He shrugged.

"Just how you did it this afternoon at Helena's would be fine. It was flawless."

He said it offhand—careless—but then looked over to me. His blue-black eyes scanned the back of my brain and that's when I knew—

"What?" Colin asked me.

"What 'what'?"

"You're looking at me funny."

"Because..." I put my drink down. The girls were still nowhere in sight. So I took the glass out of his hand, stood up, and draped his hand over my shoulder, pulling him onto the floor. "Come on."

I'd recognized the next song from the first five notes.

"I thought we weren't dancing with each other to-night." He smirked at me, and I threw my arms around him—the song drove on—the lights swam, dim—he was wearing a *suit*—and I've been able to identify every pain in my stomach since I was five years old, but—

"Ly, are you OK? You look kind of... ill."

"I am so in love with you." I knew that with the angle of my head, the roar of the dance floor, and the music blasting from the brass, there was no chance he would hear me.

"Come again?"

"It's not important."

I couldn't repeat it nor take my head away from him—he pressed his cheek against mine and I knew it then: I can't separate dancing and the movement of my body from myself—they are my entire worth, and if someone loves it and finds it beautiful, then I imagine them to be loving the best of my self, of what I have to give them. And then maybe, I can feel that it is deserved. Like that love is right. We were still dancing when some-one tapped my shoulder. Michaela, his date, was want-ing him back. I conceded, exiled myself on the barstool until Madi reappeared. She nodded when I told her I wanted to sit a few out, and drank Campari soda on a stool next to me while I watched Colin move out with Michaela to the center—

The way he twisted her body—gripped her—the way their bodies fit, her much smaller to his larger; they danced so well that the whole floor stopped to watch them.

I think that was one of the only times I could ever remember wishing I was a woman.

So that he and I could dance like that.

16

I think of Michaela's body fitting to Colin's when, next night, Valerie knocks on my door to fit her body to mine. She was gone most of last week (staying with Robert?) and I found myself almost restless at nights—was I getting used to her presence? She doesn't sleep often in my room, but lately, I can feel the hair on my arms rise with anticipation when she opens the door. And she still says nothing once she's in my bed, but since that one night, her hands haven't gone back to being still. My room is always black. She is always behind me. I don't see her face, her body. I still close my eyes—feel her hands—and I think of Cocteau's *La Belle et La Bête,* of all things. As one of my ma's favorites, I saw that movie many times when I was a kid, and was most intrigued by the hands in the beast's castle—they moved with a subtle, anonymous eroticism and that's all I see behind my eyes when Valerie moves her hands over me. The way she avoids any obvious areas, petting me with this dreamy randomness, while she never says a word to me and I never say a word to her, sets my teeth into the inside of my cheek. Until one night, I can't anymore. I'm talking to her, I know it, in my mind, *touch me, touch me, not just anywhere but...* I command her in my head, while her fingers roam—saying the words to myself over and over, as if I could hope to transfer them into her mind by the power of my will, because I can't *ask* her to do anything—that would make me complicit. And I don't want to be a *complicit* accomplice.

I don't know what I want anymore.

Another night again, she makes a line; over my shirt, from my armpit, down, her index finger catches on the ridges of my ribs, burning each one and I let out a sigh. Horrified when I realize that I'm *hard*, agonizingly so. That I want *to come*, a sensation I rarely remember feeling with someone else—even with Colin—I want him always, but it is a broader erotic feeling that encapsulates his body much more than mine—a drive that demands that I please him, or at least mutual exchange, whereas here, it's so concentrated and selfish. All of her has been reduced to a single decontextualized hand and in this void, I just want this *hand* to jerk me off—and I've never thought of myself as a sexually selfish person, or a sexual user. Am I using her? *No,* I think, *if she didn't want this, she wouldn't be doing it, right?* Is she using me? I don't know. I get tears in my eyes, from wanting it so much, and when I feel her finger again, running down my side (she must've noted the effect it had on me), I grab her by the wrist, hard and pull her hand down, but she jerks it away.

"What?!" I say then, fierce. My voice unsettles the air. I don't turn around because there is nobody to turn around to. "Why are you doing this?"

She doesn't answer; only weaves her right arm under my head, around my neck, and puts her hand on my mouth, from behind. And even that burns me, the feel of her hot hand against my lips. She keeps it there, while she reaches over to the nightstand, for the bottle of lotion that I use after showering—a big bottle, and she takes her hand off my mouth, just for a second, to put down the pump. I hear some squirt into her hand and then she puts the other hand back over my mouth, settles behind me. I lick her palm now, I want to interact with it; and she clenches it harder over me, then shoves her lotioned hand roughly between my ass-cheeks. I flinch. Remember Colin, what I had said to him when he had tried that and it was true then—even now, the thought of being penetrated disgusts me—she does it quickly though, without speaking, without asking, or permission, and I'm surprised by the sensation. It's uncomfortable at first, a slick, hot finger—

I squirm to get away, and she talks then, so low and soft that I'm not even sure if she's really saying it, or if it's a voice in my head.

It's what you wanted, isn't it?

You like it, don't you?

"Don't talk to me," I growl, and she doesn't anymore, just pumps her finger into me, until I start to like it. I want it, but it's on the most base and physical level—if I could think clearly, it might be different, but she starts touching some spot—rubbing it—

She doesn't touch me anywhere else and I don't touch myself; I bite the inside of my mouth bloody; and I've never had an orgasm feel this—long—internal—radiating out from somewhere deep inside. I don't want to give it to her or to myself, but nothing will stop it. She keeps her finger in me, pressing on that spot; the other anonymous hand releases my mouth— strokes my face while I come and come—

"Oh Ly," she whispers. "Keep coming. Keep going. You're so beautiful."

The next morning, Valerie comes into the kitchen while I'm getting my nonfat yogurt out of the fridge. She microwaves a cup of water for instant coffee. Both of us have circles under our eyes.

I sit and she chatters about the meeting she will have with the college board today regarding a student accused of plagiarism—then presses her fingertips into her eyelids dramatically.

"Sorry I keep yawning. I'm so exhausted. I barely slept at all last night."

I know! I want to scream. *I was there!*

She swallows a sip of coffee and dabs her thin, ugly little lips with a paper towel. Her eyes are round, dull and shiny, as always. Trashed bottle caps winking on the side of the road. Short arms, bulky shoulders, breasts misshapen, lumpy from a badly chosen bra—looking at the crudely formed totality of her features in the light of day repulses me. *YOU made me feel that way?* In the morning, everything about her is so wrong—and what happened in the unknown dark no longer seems glamorously, mysteriously filthy. *Just* filthy.

She waves noncommittally.

"All right. I gotta get ready for work. See you later."

My wave back is tepid.

Today's split is complete.

17

The next weekend, Colin took me to the Candy Club, a cruisy little place where we both love the dance floor, and on Saturday nights they have the best DJ. We decided to go out for a last huzzah because I was leaving at the end of the next week, to go back to California for Christmas. I spent the afternoon at Helena's working on my audition piece, then we went out to the Charles because I wanted to see the state of our outdoor stage, but he'd told me it wouldn't be close to ready. I was excited for my first real winter, but it had yet to be cold enough. We'd just had our first snow. So we drove back home, to get ready to go out.

That night in the club, I was feeling abstracted—or maybe its complete opposite, driven. I don't know, but I had the look for it. We were on the dance floor, him and I—I wouldn't dance with anyone else, and we didn't do anything fancy, just good old fashioned dirty dancing where I ground against him until his fingers gripped the back of my neck. I wrapped my body around him until he dragged me to the bar—

"Are you trying to get us arrested for indecent behavior?"

"I think we're wearing too much for that." I sipped

my soda and traced a finger down his neck, knowing that drives him crazy—Colin closed his eyes. Finished his soda in two gulps, coughing out, "Let's go."

And I was fine with that—I wanted him to want me enough to force it. All through the afternoon, it was all I could do to keep myself from asking and deferring to what I imagined to be his superior body of experience, but what kind of questions would I even ask? "Have you ever enjoyed anonymous sex that wasn't really anonymous... or necessarily sex? Was it sex? Oh, important detail; it was with a woman." Then I told myself I was getting crazier than a shithouse*cat* for even *thinking* about telling him.

"Whose place?" he asked once we got in the car, and didn't wait for my answer. "Mine. It's closer."

He zoomed down Storrow, then crossed the black river. Colin lives closer to Cambridge than to downtown Boston and I love his apartment: a cozy, beautiful studio, off a small street near Mass Ave. We were lucky that night, there was a spot close to his building. He parallel parks like no other—almost pulled me up the stairs, then pushed his door open. I pushed him in, and up against the wall—our breathing was ragged—good, I thought, happy by how much I wanted it, but did I want it like—?

Candelabras. Floating white hands.

Stop.

He drew a hand down my side, made me groan, and I kept my eyes closed, not wanting to see his expression that might have been questioning. An expression that said: *What's gotten into you tonight? This isn't like you.*

But I wanted it to be. He pushed me on the bed. Colin's body was behind me, over me, he pressed into me from the back while he sucked my neck—I knew I was going to bruise from his mouth, I could tell and normally, he wasn't pushy, but that night, he was fighting to check himself. When I felt one of his hands clutch my lower back, the other my neck, I grabbed at it; pulled down. Signaled that I wanted to say something to him.

He lowered his right ear to me.

"Yes?"

"I want you to," I told him and he touched my cheekbone.

"...What?"

"I said, I want you to."

He sat on my lower back, smoothed his body over me, until his face was by mine. *I couldn't see him* and I closed my eyes. Please don't think about white hands. Please don't think about...

"Ly, this is your first time, no?"

No words, just a nod. He opened a drawer in his nightstand. Took something out, started saying it would be cold, but he'd need to use a lot to make sure it didn't hurt. I felt him pour something, yes it was cold and wet, more on himself, and he massaged me for a few minutes, then carefully inserted a finger—it felt strange again, like forced entry, and after a while, I got used to it, *but does it feel good?*, then the logistical crinkling of wrappers, he put himself against me—bent over my back again, kissing me between the shoulder blades. That made me shudder, I don't know why, I preferred that from him, I almost wanted to tell him—no, I changed my mind... please... use your mouth—He put it to my ear.

"Are you sure about this? I don't have to do it."

"Yes, you do," I mumbled, which was not the same as saying, "I want it to happen," and he ran his hands along me—my hesitation was making him hesitate. But he also wanted to too much to think more about it.

"Try to breathe."

I did as he said—

He grabbed my shoulder hard, and both of us inhaled sharply when it went in—

"...*Fuck*..." he muttered under his breath, and I clenched, seeing my knuckles whiten as I gripped the edge of the mattress. I felt my face whiten, drained of blood, my lips whiten, when they released the sound:

"*Owww...*"

"Come on," Colin moaned. I'd never heard anyone sound like him right then, except myself, the other night: had she made me sound like this? Someone completely consumed. "Come on, it can't be that bad..."

"Yes, it can; it fucking hurts," I snarled, and he massaged my shoulder blades with his slicked hands, then bent low over me like a jockey on a horse. Unable to see my face, I'm not sure if he got what I said, but he read my back's tension well.

"You said you wanted me to. So do you want me to stop now?"

I said nothing.

"Ly, should I stop?"

He was moaning and trembling, I could tell he completely did not want.

To stop.

I shook my head.

"I'll go really slow." He talked to me, lightening his strokes, while he massaged my shoulders. "Relax... relax..."

At some point, I felt a turning point, like my body had accepted him, and it started to feel more pleasurable, but always with an undercurrent of pain. He made me get on my knees so he could touch me, and I finally came, but it wasn't the same—I knew it wasn't and afterwards, I felt as empty as a bottle. We showered and then fell asleep and I had a convoluted dream, involving white hands. But we slept facing each other; he put his arms around me—I could look at him if I wanted. And sometimes in the night, I kissed Colin; sometimes, he me. That I liked.

18

I imagine someone trapped in a cycle of dancing dances with beginnings but no endings. I think of stories again, of the story of dancing, while I dance in my room. Sometimes just stretching: easy movements, light turns—there's only my bed, which is a double. No desk, a single shelf (for my wallet and keys, and a framed picture of us back home: Russ, Ma and me, smiling wide some years back, at Cannery Row). A small stereo. A hardwood floor that gets so cold, but I resist putting a rug over it because I use the small space—it's a constrained space. I put on music and dance out of confusion, thinking more lately of a mode of storytelling

I've never much considered until now. Maybe sex is the dance of restraints? I know that if I tell Valerie to stop coming, I will never know the ending of this story.

She comes into my room two nights later and settles into my bed. Neither of us speaks. The only sound I hear is her pumping lotion onto her hand—I can't deny it. I'm so excited, I almost strain for her, and I breathe out a sigh when I feel her fingers on me, when she starts to stroke my skin—

"Do you want me to touch you?" I ask her then, quietly, and she puts her hand over my mouth again.

"I have some requirements, you know. One is that *you* can't talk."

"Why?" I whisper, muffled behind her hand. "Why do you get to call all the shots?"

"Because—" She puts her index finger deep in me, to the knuckle, and I exhale. "—You don't want to touch me."

I clench and don't argue, thinking, true? Not true, probably true, yes it's true, who cares, yes, you can say anything, do anything to me, *just don't stop.* I don't know if she's a queen petting her slave—or a slave petting her prince—the ghost never kisses me and I'm right on the brink, when she says, "You don't want me, or any woman. So you don't have to pretend to be considerate."

"Do you..." I grit my teeth. "Get anything out of this?"

"Don't... *talk*..." And she presses that spot inside again—I start to come, which she likes, I know, I feel her push into me from behind, the wetness of her through her thin shirt. And it's a painful orgasm, because it's incomplete; I spasm without satisfaction—

"Your mouth... please..." I gasp and I feel her shake her head.

"No. You don't get to tell me what to do. You don't get to *see* me."

"Please..."

She pulls herself out of me, turns herself around now. For once she is facing the wall. Valerie's slipped off her underwear, but her shirt is still on and I turn around and have my arms around her, pressing into her from behind.

"Here..." is all she says, pushing her ass against my groin, and I blush at the implication—does she imagine that's what I naturally prefer? Still, after all this time of not wanting it, my hesitation is so momentary; right now, I need to penetrate something. Something, I think—do I even care if it's her or someone else? *What is going on?* I lube myself up and she gives me no instruction or warning, so I press into her, trying to be careful, but instantly I understand Colin's predicament. The pressure is so tight that I seize a corner of the mattress to keep from coming right away, to keep from hurting her. No, I don't think of her as a her, even when I move my arms around to the front of her body. Her shirt has ridden up. I've never touched a woman's naked body before and I avoid her breasts—put off by the idea of soft, excess flesh—I move my right hand lower. Her stomach is round; it feels soft and pleasant to touch, my finger is in her navel, then lower; that nub—it fascinates me; how she moans when I brush it, lightly rub it—finally, I end all the way down—slip a finger into her, shocked by how wet it is, but not disgusted; I probably would have been under other circumstances, but without seeing it, it seems as innocent as a mouth sucking on my finger, and I fall into a trance until I hear her speak.

"Make me come."

"How?" I shudder—no idea—these parts seem so complicated—but she whispers,

"It's not hard at all. You just have to say my name."

I stroke into her deep, biting my lip. Thinking the most random thoughts: *Say my name, Bastian!* Another never-ending story... and the inappropriate memory almost makes me laugh, but then I come back. Break it down. I just have to say.

Her name:

Valerie.

Va

le

rie.

Kind of flowery.

I have the same visceral aversion to putting it on my tongue as I do to touching her breasts.

"I can't..."

"Why not?"

"Because it's a girl's name... it would..."

Ruin everything. She knows and laughs at me.

"It doesn't have to be a girl's name, you know. We had a student some years back. He was from Ukraine, and his name was Valeriy. He said it was a common masculine name in his country. Valeriy. With a 'y'. Pretend." Her ass grips me and I stifle a noise into her back. My hands feel hot and trapped.

Valeriy.

I hear the name in a language more like my mother's: huskier, throaty—no longer floral, all victory or valor and now I imagine her as a male. I wonder if I could be attracted to her if she were a man. Close-cropped blond hair and those hard, dull eyes—the color of a rifle's barrel. She wouldn't have big, misshapen breasts then, her stocky body would be more muscular. Her broad shoulders would fit.

And I start to imagine—my finger is still in him, then another. Then I feel one of his hands go down—he takes my hand, pulling me out of him and into an anesthetized dream of my own finger being traced against my neck—cheek—that's when I tremble—. Like fish, like sea, like salty milk, like dirty coins, like wet dog; like a hundred things I've heard described since junior high in steaming locker rooms as alternately revolting or erotic. My hand freezes right before the finger touches my lips—I neither like nor hate the smell, only feel it paralyze me with the strange perfume that has now soaked into my sheets and skin. I'll never get it out, and if I meet Colin tomorrow, will he know, instantly? *This is not me. This is not me. What am I doing here?* Terror—an awful dread soaks through me. He feels my hesitation, but takes my fingers back down, presses against the back of my hand—pushes me into him, deeper, deeper; lightly gasps into my pillow.

"Is it as disgusting as you always imagined?"

Starts to laugh, softly, over his moan. And I fuck him harder now, as hard as I want to, without consideration, and with each thrust (b i t c h)—plow into him front and back—until I can touch my own body through his, until I make him groan, deep and pained... A man's groan. God, that time when he says my name ([*lisand·ʒɛ*] *perfect pronunciation*) I don't think I'll ever forget it. He says it like the filthiest word I've ever heard.

And no matter how hard I grip him around the stomach, how hard I try, I can't hurt him. How could I, when I've never needed anything more than the next five seconds when he finally dumps me into him. I can't hold it back then—my mouth is against his neck and I talk to him like he asked me to and like he didn't ask me to.

"Valeriy. Valeriy... Oh—what the fuck have you done to me..."

19

Christmas was only a week away.

Colin invited me to spend a few days at his family's house before I flew back to LA for the holidays. The day before I left found us in Filene's, fighting over the last pieces of merchandise with aggressive geriatric shoppers. That was the mission because he still hadn't found his favorite aunt a present. Eventually settling on a pair of earrings, we were about to leave when I suddenly remembered and asked if he would mind going to the sleepwear department with me. He didn't, and I went looking through the pajamas—after much deliberation, I finally narrowed it down to two. One was midnight blue, checked. The other a deep moss green, with very touchable, soft fabric. I held them up, side by side.

"If you were a girl, which one of these would you like more?"

Colin raised his eyebrows.

"Who are you getting *pajamas* for, anyway? Isn't it too hot to wear them in California?"

"I'm not getting them for anyone in my family. I'm getting them for my roommate. Valerie."

His mouth twisted a little.

"You're buying a Christmas present for the weird girl?"

I felt defensive, but checked it.

"She's really not that bad. I never did get close to anyone else in my house—her and I talk pretty often. And she always complains about being too cold at night."

He put his arms around me then and planted a light kiss on my forehead, making me blush.

"You have a keen sense of responsibility—but she should blame her boyfriend if she's cold at night. Get the green."

We had the gifts wrapped at the wrapping station, then walked around downtown, drinking hot chocolate and taking in Christmas lights. Said good night at Park Station. I needed to pack that night if I was to go over to Colin's the next afternoon.

"Alright. See you tomorrow."

I got on the T and went home. The apartment was empty when I arrived and I wished then that I had not refused Colin's offer to go have dinner together, even if it guilted me to see him pay for a full meal I would barely eat any of. Still, the kitchen was so cold and dreary, I started to formulate an early New Year's resolution: to paint the walls some color other than this dank gray. Aubergine? Too dark, I thought. Mint? I was drinking tea and eating cut-up apples by the table when I heard the front door open and I knew it had to be Valerie, because Michael and Mira had already left to join their families the day before. We'd be the only ones here tonight, barring she didn't bring Robert over, but no, she was alone when she came in, off to her room with her nose buried in some blockbuster novel.

And tears coming down her face.

She didn't even see me as she walked past.

"Hey, Valerie. What's wrong?" I stopped her and she put the book down. Focused her grey eyes on me.

"Nothing. Well, yeah, I guess something. But not really."

108

"Do you want some tea? Want to talk about it?"

I offered her a seat and she put the book further away from her. Seemed to be considering if she wanted to talk or go hole up in her room, but finally, she breathed in deep. Exhaled.

"I guess I can tell you. Robert broke up with me. Or I guess, I broke up with him."

My body stiffened, and I almost burned myself taking the hot water out from the microwave.

"...You broke up? Why?"

She shrugged. "I guess, I felt like he wasn't being quite honest with me lately. And I confronted him about it and after being shifty forever, he finally came clean and told me that yeah. His parents were never going to agree to us getting married. Never in a million years. They think he can do better, and he doesn't want to go against them and risk anything regarding his inheritance. Which is when I told him that he was a coward, and that he should've told me earlier and that I didn't want to see him again." She leaned back in her seat, her face as eerily blank as a wet egg. "I don't know. Maybe I was too hasty, but the way I see it, I'm at the age where I don't really have time to be *with guys who are only interested in having fun.*"

I swallowed, but she just looked past me, placid almost—with such an empty remoteness that I wondered if she had some kind of psychological *condition* that allowed her to selectively and completely forget other parts of herself in any given time or situation. If I was anything to her beyond a roommate-acquaintance that she sometimes one-sidedly talked to over tea, I would never have known it from any gesture or expression on her face right then.

"I'm sorry," I muttered, isolated in my awkwardness that seemed entirely unshared, and she looked at me. Smiled feebly, then raised her mug to clink with mine.

"It's not your fault. I'll find someone else. That's life, I guess."

"Well." I stared out the window. "I didn't like him anyway. You are too good for him."

I jumped up before she could say anything and ran to my room, remembering. Came back a minute later.

"What's this?" she asked when I pressed the wrapped package into her hands.

"Something I said I'd get you a while back. I know I'm a week early, but I'm leaving tomorrow so... this will be my last chance before Christmas to give it to you."

She opened the package and took out the pajamas and for maybe a second, her features betrayed *something*. I remembered her reaction when I had brought her take-out that time in the fall—would she cry now? But I guess she was already crying. She looked up at me and squeezed my lower arm.

"Aww. Thanks, hon. That's really considerate. I'm sorry. I didn't think to get anything for you."

"It's fine. It was random that I remembered anyway."

She buried her face in the flannel's soft material, drying a few tears for Robert on it, then looked up again.

"You know, you shouldn't be so nice."

"What's wrong with being nice?" I smiled.

She smiled back.

"Nothing. It's just unnecessarily confusing."

20

I know he's going to come tonight. I know it. I lie in bed waiting, listening to the snow falling outside. Snow that falls in a silence so thick, you swear you can hear it. The clock says two and I want him to not appear. I want to fall asleep, so I do what I do when I can't sleep—recreate my favorite dances in my head—the steps from shows I love—choreographies—I think about the dance for the audition in front of the Conservatory board—the clock says three—I consider getting up and going out on a walk, maybe getting a hot drink at the twenty-four-hour convenience store four blocks over, just to have an aim. The door opens.

I stop breathing.

He slips into bed, crawling over my body to get behind by the wall, and every muscle in me is already at breaking point—already, it's enough. Already, I am wanting him. This must be what it feels like to go insane, I think, while I stare out at the room with my back to him, like always, while he puts his body to mine, fitting his softness to me, and tonight, I want to talk. I will insist on it.

I say, "It's so late, I thought you weren't coming."

"Why would I not come? It's our last night."

"Don't say that."

"But it's true?"

He puts his fingers on my neck, on my back under my shirt and I put my left hand behind me, to try to touch him—

He pushes it away.

"Why can't I ever touch you?" I whisper.

"Don't talk."

"Why?"

"Because."

"Because why? Do you like using me?"

He laughs, cutting.

"If you feel used, I can leave." Starts to move and I grab his arm.

"Please…"

"Please what?"

"Please don't leave."

"Then don't talk."

I close my mouth, helpless. Somehow, here, always, he has all the control, and I don't know what to say or how to change that. He pulls off my clothes, takes lotion again. I think I'll have to throw away this bottle and get a new scent because this smell is now permanently linked in my mind with this. He makes his hands hot and slippery and pulls off the covers—I lay there, shivering, not opening my eyes—blackness is all there is and a phosphorescent white hand—and he sits up next to me. The bed shifts—he touches me everywhere now—behind the ear—under the collarbones—traces my abs—rubs a finger between my big and second toe, up over the high arch of my foot—

"I wasn't going to leave anyway." Now a gentler tone. "But I meant it when I told you, you shouldn't be so nice." His fingers graze my body and I don't move my hand to him. I know he's studying me—perhaps thinking that this is the first time something said during the day has been acknowledged in the night.

For once, day and night collapse.

"Oh, I wish sometimes," he says.

"What?"

"Shh."

I lick my lips, lock them, then hear his voice again—full of the disembodied sorrow of people who speak in their sleep with nobody to hear them.

"I wish that..."

Not daring to talk, I put my hand out, try to find one of his fingers—but he ignores any contact—I hear for eternity the blacknoise of no touching, then the next sensation is a fingertip drawn down the bridge of my nose.

"I meant it," he says again. "It does no good to be good, Lysandrze."

So much time has passed that my whole body prickles up from hearing him say my name. I want to ask him to say it again, but I know I shouldn't break it. Valeriy stays silent, and I turn my face towards him, eyes still closed, but I smile. Figuring that at least must be allowed, but it is a mistake.

His hand stops.

"Put it in," he says then, suddenly, as if he has realized the slip. Maybe I should be upset at this sudden shift, but it just makes me moan. I turn to him and open my eyes only after he's rotated to the wall—looking freely now at his broad, wax-white back. His thin, almost white blond hair splashed on my pillow. I put my chin on his shoulder.

Lube up, then slip into him, fighting to not push too hard when my body wants all of it right away. He cries out, loud this time, muffling himself almost instantly in my pillow—I think again of when Colin did it to me—

"Does it hurt?" I whisper and he shakes his head, hiccups—Still, I stroke his lower stomach, not moving at all, letting him adjust, but he tells me to keep going, so I do, until his whimpers turn into moans. He rolls onto his stomach and I'm above him. All the way, he tells me, so I do it. My stomach is tensed flat against his back; and I grab him around the torso. He takes the fingers of my right hand, bites them—do I feel good to him? I don't know—I wish I did, but all I can sense is his suffering—

"Valeriy." I press a kiss on the back of his neck. "I know you don't like hearing my voice, but I have to talk now, because you have to come soon... because I can't anymore... so please. *Valeriy.*"

"Ly." His eyes are closed, face is turned to the side on my pillow, maybe the only time I've seen it really clearly since he's been coming at night—he looks beautiful to me then, like a curvy boy, or an exhausted angel, and the way he talks cuts me throat to navel. "I do like hearing your voice though."

"...You do?"

"Yes. I love how you say my name."

"How?" I murmur, while I feel his body give it up to me, inch by aggressive inch, cell by cell—like mine gives it up to his.

"You say it like you love fucking me." He sucks my finger, then bites it as delicately as a kitten, while the rest of him clenches white blood out of me. "*You say it like you love me.*"

It's not in to love it, but I'm a fan of LA—the smog, the acres of dystopian cracked concrete—the synthetic smiles, breasts, attitudes. I love those things, like the sun, the palm trees, the open air shimmering in the heat. Colin and I were talking about our life goals one night when I told him that I could see myself moving back to LA once I was done with the East Coast. Join a company, then teach or choreograph eventually. He seemed surprised.

"Everyone I've met from LA so far has acted like they'd crawled out of the Inferno."

"Well, not me. It's beautiful, in its own way."

"They say there are no seasons, though."

"Yeah. No *shitty* seasons." I grinned and he tousled my hair.

"Alright. If you say so. I was there once for a show, but I didn't have much time to look around. I could go with you sometime and you could show me some places. Be my Virgil."

I used to imagine our first trip to LA together. He'd fall in love with it too and want to stay there with me forever, but that conversation was so long ago.

Who knows if he remembers it still.

My plane landed a little after five in the evening. I got off the flight feeling fresh, having slept almost the whole way. My ma met me by arrivals and I really was so happy to see her—she'd even dressed up, with that touch of

Doris Day about her hair. I couldn't stop myself: it felt like it had been years, not half of one, and I grabbed her by the waist and swung her in a swing move—Around the World. One of her butter-colored pumps flew off her foot and skittered under some seats.

She screeched, "You nut!"

Then we hugged and I retrieved her shoe and slipped it back on her foot.

"I like your dress."

"Oh stop. This dress is so old." She kissed me on the cheek and fingered the collar of my heavy East Coast jacket, which I'd already had to remove—it was sixty degrees, almost forty-five degrees warmer than when I'd left Boston six hours ago. "You look wonderful." Momspeak for, "You don't look like you're starving to death," because she knows how touchy my stomach is and how I can lose weight alarmingly fast. "Have you been eating better, then?"

"Pretty good, Ma." I smiled.

"I worry so much about you being there all alone."

"I'm not alone, though. I've got someone to take care of me."

She didn't look at me, only pulled me towards the baggage carousel, and I saw her try to wipe a few tears surreptitiously while she made to grab my bag (that's the one, isn't it, honey?).

My ma seemed so small then, coming only to my chest. I kissed the top of her head and pulled my bag over to the car. She drove us home. Dinner that night was potato pancakes (one of the few standbys of Polish cuisine that doesn't threaten my life) and we sat around in the kitchen, drinking tea and talking until early in the morning—

My mom and I have always had good, long discussions, but despite the length, this one managed to feel truncated and untrue. I didn't tell her about the upcoming audition and the Conservatory, because I didn't want her to worry, to pray and fret—so I carried on about Helena and my students. And though I wished I could tell her about Colin, I didn't want to see a certain expression come on her face and ruin it all, so he was curiously absent from my stories too. Then the next day, we met with my brother Russell—his wife and their first kid (another kid due in two months, unbelievable how mature Russell the Ass has gotten)—and the days went by with walks in the neighborhood, driving down to the beach. Enjoying the winter sun. And a lot of un-thinking.

The week was almost over when I went over to Trischa's for my hair. Once upon a time, Trischa Bu and I had been two kids obsessed with ballet, pounding the junior circuits together. Our bodies had been identical slips of gummy earthworm twisting into fantastic shapes, ready to freak any adult out by pretzeling our heels behind our ears. Then puberty hit. My neurotic stomach was perfect for maintaining my earthworm form, but Trischa suffered. Is it crazy that I like this? she would ask me in her sister's bedroom, preening in front of the vanity mirror. Her chubby hands resting on her roundening hips. The world was deep in heroin chic, so yes, people thought she was crazy. But Trischa was simply ahead of her time. I'm not dancing anymore, Ly. I remember when she told me. Not as a career, anyway. That all is messed up. I'm not participating. But she stayed in the scene, as a makeup artist and costume maker.

Trischa and I went through it together. In dance circles, we were so ordinary; in school, we were freak-flowers growing out beyond the perimeters, faces both blooming with acne, waiting to accelerate into our-selves. The kids at school didn't accept us, but we didn't need them to.

Trisch's mom ran a beauty salon out of a converted ga-rage space on the ground floor of their home, and my ma would go over sometimes and pay to get her grays touched up. I grew up welcome at the Bu's, as Trischa was at our place as well—relations only got strained the year that Trischa came out and changed her name to Trischa. Both of us got caught in the crossfire. Mrs. Bu told my mother that surely it was the influence of a soft boy best friend who had made her child become this way, and my mother had shot back that at least her own son was 'only' gay, which was still in some, how-ever undesirable, range of 'normal.' We were mutually banned from each other's houses for half a year at least, and Trisch and I were forced to go clandestine in the neighborhood playground if we wanted to meet.

But that is ancient history.

Now I sat in their garage's salon chair with a towel around my neck, while Trischa smeared the noxious-smelling bleach into my roots. I'd gotten to dyeing and toning my hair myself in Boston (no way could I afford a professional), but Trischa was willing to give me the Old Friend Discount. Doing my hair was also a good venue for both of us to get in some free therapy; she was expounding, as she smeared, on this awful boyfriend of hers who had been cheating on her for months before he finally had the balls to confess himself—and then, she continued, he had the nerve to try to beg for her forgiveness with an unbelievably unbelievable story of why the unfaithfulness had happened.

"Jeez, Ly, I mean, you're a guy, but you're still trustworthy." Her hand stopped for a moment. "Can you explain this to me?"

And I felt a stone in my stomach, because the person she was addressing was the person who had left LA last summer—and things I've had the luxury of not having to think of for the last week suddenly crowded to the fore of my brain. She kept talking.

"Oh, but wait a minute. It's pointless to even talk to you about this because you are *so in love* right now with that Colin, you can't empathize with my dating problems. Which reminds me. I've been hearing you gush over him for the last three months but still haven't seen his picture—I'm starting to think you made him up."

"I did NOT. There's a picture of him in my bag right now, if you want to see it. I took one from his room right before I left. It's in my planner."

"I think I'll do that."

Putting the plastic bowl of deep purple solution down, she snapped off her gloves, grabbed my messenger bag, picked through—got the planner—

"The front flap," I told her. "There are some post-cards, and it's there. I think..." I heard her rummage—pages flipping—then.

"Holy moly."

"What?" I was wondering what unspeakable item she'd found tucked in the front flap of my planner, but Trisch only waved the photo at me. It was a pic I had filched from a shoebox I had found in his old room, filled with various shots of him and friends and dancers and backstages. This one was Colin sitting with his arm around some dancer in an exploded dressing room—jeans, white shirt, looking off somewhere—an unlit cig-arette in his full mouth—a girl's hand coming in from the right of the frame to light it—(apparently, he was a smoker until just last year, when he started developing a bad cough and quit cold turkey). I remember when my fingers first grabbed this candid photo out of a pile of perfectly arranged shots—

I was staring at the picture so intently that Colin looked over, so I quickly flicked to the next ones, but that impression was impossible to erase.

It was hard to explain, but seeing him like that, as if for the first time again, made me realize—that some people have in their beauty, or grace, or fluidity, their talent—something that kisses divinity. And the rest of us are condemned to be blinded by it. To long for, but never touch it. I knew then—Colin could let me talk to him, share his thoughts with me, let me sleep with him, penetrate my body or let me penetrate his. I could have listened to every secret in his soul, then cut his abdo-men open and embraced his warm-beating organs individually—but I could not have possessed whatever it was that made him blinding. This obsessed me— And I knew that someone like him could never understand, which is why I wanted this one picture so much. I looked through all of them, then came back to it, and I asked him to give it to me.

"Sure, if you want, but there are much better ones in that pile."

"No, I like this one. Sign it please, on the back."

He smiled and wrote on it for me and I put the picture away thinking—whatever happens, I'll always have this.

"So this is him." Trischa was reading the inscription on the back.

"Yeah. That's him."

She started kissing the picture with luscious smacks—"mwah mwah MWAH"—and I felt more deflated than ever.

"Wauuuu, what a gorg darling. And tell me, how did you get this guy to even look at you?"

"Gee thanks. Guess now I know you think I'm a dog."

"Come on, Ly. You've got fabulous hair and legs like a gazelle, but your skin is a mess and you and him are not playing in the same league. Or let me guess." She pulled on new gloves and continued smearing. "The dark beauty is a dish best enjoyed *silent*, because all the good genes went to the exterior and he has like, two brain cells fighting for domination."

"Not at all."

"Is he pretentious?"

"He's smart, but not enough to be annoying."

"That's good. Is he an asshole? Controlling?"

"He's really nice."

"...But does he fuck you proper?"

I turned salmon—Trischa met me in the mirror.

"You haven't changed a bit. Still my prude little pseudo-Christian catboy. Congrats then. Of course he had to be gay. But it looks like you have found the last decent man in the United States of America. You won't get this lucky again, so don't screw it up."

"Trischa."

"Mmm?"

I just said it:

"I'm cheating on my gorgeous boyfriend who loves me with a strange, ugly woman who loves to get fucked by me. And I don't know how to stop."

Her hands stopped mid-smear.

"I feel like I'm missing... a lot here."

So I filled her in. And I could tell that she didn't quite know what to do with it once I got to the end, like I didn't know what to do with it, so she jumped on the most obvious plot-hole.

"I guess you're into women now?"

"I'm NOT, Trisch, this is what makes it so messed up! I'm not into *her* either—I mean, we're friendly in the apartment, but she's almost forty—entitled—*conservative*—we don't have anything in common. I unironically think that she's a terrible human being. We went out together to see a show once and it was a disaster, but ever since she started coming into my bed... I don't know, something about the way she touches me turns me on so *fucking* much, that I can't give it up. We don't even talk in bed—she doesn't want me to. I don't see her face, she doesn't look at mine—we've never kissed each other—not on the lips, not on the cheek—nowhere. I have a hard time believing in the morning that it's the same person, because by day, she wears suits and goes to an office and drinks venti lattes and acts like an uptight middle-aged binch and like absolutely nothing is going on between us. But at night, it's dark—it's like she could be anyone—she acts different—talks different—and I usually... actually... pretend she's a guy..."

Youch!

Trischa had put the bowl down and slugged me on the shoulder.

"What was that for?!" I squirmed in the seat.

"That's for being a complete idiot. I mean, what is wrong with you?"

She dropped a comb. I winced from the clatter and bent over to pick it up for her.

"Sorry." Her hands kept moving, but I could see her face in the mirror. "No offense Ly, but that's sick and messed up. I can't believe you're one of those gross guys who fucks a woman he's ashamed of on the DL."

If she hadn't been bleaching my hair, I would have bent over to cover my face. I could feel my gullet tighten.

"She practically forces me to!"

"That doesn't make sense. And you said you liked it? Be honest. You like it, you're just *ashamed* that you like it. God, you're seriously no better than my rotten ex!"

"I know. I know! I should come clean and confess everything to him. Right? He'd know what to do."

She whacked me again.

"Ok, now you're being goddamn STUPID. Why the hell would you *tell* him?"

"Because you told me that your boyfriend had confessed to you, and that he explained the extenuating circumstances, and..."

"And you think I gave a damn for his pathetic excuses? Heck no! *I dumped him!* So confessing is a great idea, if you want the Last Decent Man in America to dump you. I'll be blunt though: it would be right for him to. You don't deserve him, Ly."

And I remembered then my goodbye from Colin, in his bedroom in his parents' apartment.

We lay in bed, kissing (clean, beautiful sheets) and talked about the audition, and how excited he was that I was finally doing it. If I made it, I would be in a temporary probation program, but once I was out of that, I would most likely be able to accelerate my classes— And I got that scorch in my heart again—that fear—that he liked me too much—that I didn't deserve him—that I hadn't earned him—in fact, that I was destroying my right to be loved by him more and more all the time.

Colin sat up.

"You were staring off with this expression right now. You all right?"

"No... I mean, it's the audition. I'm thinking about it all the time."

"You're worried about it."

I said nothing, letting my silence fill in an implied 'yes.'

He nodded, stood up, walked to his CD player.

"Well, when I'm worried, you know what always cheers me up?"

I smiled at him weakly and rolled out of bed. Watched him come to me—lithe, sleek—he took the lead—and when he twirled me in the rhumba—when our bodies met, I knew then; when he put me to the ground and I felt his movement in my spine—

Maybe this is what I was expecting.

And so I sat in front of Trischa, remembering all that and getting bathed in unrighteous sadness. It wasn't because I wanted her pity and I certainly didn't want my own, but I couldn't help it.

"Aww, Jesus, Ly. I know it's asking a lot, but don't cry. I'm sorry I said that, but... don't."

She put the bowl down, looked at my roots, and made a satisfied sound—then snapped off her gloves again.

"I can't hug you right now. That bleach smells so strong."

My tears were running down.

"You're so right, Trisch. I don't deserve him. And I've been thinking that all along."

"Oh, shh. That was harsh of me to say. But so do you want advice? Or should I keep my mouth shut?"

"Advice, please."

"Alright. Here's your plan. Promise yourself right now that it won't happen again—repeat that often and firmly believe it. Then when you get back to Boston, the first thing you do is face her. During the day, before anything weird comes up. Tell her it will never happen again. Do whatever you have to do. Lock your door. And then make sure it never happens again. And then forget about it. But DO NOT tell him. And do not, under any circumstances, cheat on that beautiful man again, because if you do, as sure as God made little green apples—you'll be spending time in a very special and particularly horrible circle of Hell." She gave me some Kleenex. "Do you promise me you'll do that?"

"Yeah."

"Cross your heart and hope to die? Stick a needle in your eye? Keep your fork because there's pie?"

"I promise."

She squeezed my shoulder, careful to avoid my head.

"Ok, good. I want you to call me when you're back in Boston, right after you tell her."

22

I arrive back in Boston on a subzero Monday—humming Tori Amos's cover of "I Don't Like Mondays" as I navigate through Logan and make my way down to the T station. Drag my big bag onto the train and watch myself in the dark pools of the windows—Trischa really went suicide on my hair, and now I look like a wayward surfer who maybe should've never gotten off that plane. Once the color settles a bit, I'll dye it something else.

Back in Sommerville, I slalom my bag over the bumps of snow around the curbs, finally making it to our apartment. I let myself in and the TV's emitting, making me wonder if I'm ready for my promised talk with Valerie to happen this quick, but no—it's not her. Michael's the one stretched out on one of the couches in his sweat pants, socked feet on the low table, drinking a coffee. I put my bag into my room then go in to say a quick hello.

"Oh hey, Ly. Welcome back," he says.

"Thanks. You have a nice vacation?"

"Sure. Not as good as yours I bet, down in Cali-four-nigh-aye. But fair enough. Saw the whole crew and all."

"That's nice. Is everyone else back too?"

He takes a sip from his mug.

"Mira's back, but Valerie's took off."

"Oh, where to?"

"Actually." He sits up now and takes his feet off of the coffee table. "I was hoping you could tell me."

I don't like the way he's looking at me—with a furtive, extortionist's leer. He leans back again on the couch and lazily scratches his proto pot-belly through his stained shirt, which makes me feel prissy. I'm thinking, eww. Mike says:

"I know you've heard me bitch about her a couple times before, but this time, she's really put herself *high* on my shit list. She's AWOL."

"What do you mean, AWOL?"

"Like gone. Like she moved her crap out and took off. And she owes me for a month of rent that she borrowed last month. And she never paid this month's. Promised she would, right when we met again after Christmas. Said her family always gave her a lot of money for the holidays and she would have it. Then I come back and I see that all her shoes and shit that she kept in the hall are gone. I thought that was strange, so I went into her room, and that place was *cleared out*. There wasn't a sock left—no note, no nothing. Checked my email. My spam folders. Nothing."

I hope my face isn't chalking out. But I suspect it is. He goes on.

"So I wanted to ask if you know anything about it, or where she might've gone. Otherwise, I'm out of a chunk of cash, and you and me and Mira are swallowing her last month's rent as well. Not to mention this month's, if we don't find a replacement soon."

"I don't... know. Anything."

Mike looks pissed, as if he's sure I'm hiding something. A slow, greasy grin spreads across his face.

"Come on, Ly. She must've told you *something*. I mean, I know you were fucking her."

I don't know what I look like from hearing him say that, but it must not be good, because he puts his hands up in front of himself, palms out.

"Look, no judgment. It's none of my business, which is why I never mentioned it until now, but the point is, you knew her better than anyone in this house, so if you have another email or number for her, other than the ones she's been ignoring, I would really appreciate it."

He throws me a challenging glare. Perhaps he's waiting for me to deny our relationship, or to finally cough up a number—but I won't do the first, and I never got the second from her. Nor a goodbye, not even a warning. And I don't know what I feel. Is it relief, that the problem is now *gone?* Am I happy for this unexpected development? Part of me is, sure. Because it means I'm out of this mess I've landed myself in, cleanly, suddenly and completely. But then I remember his voice—right then, standing in the living room in front of the coffee table—I remember the way just hearing him say my name in bed could turn me inside out—

I shiver, like I'd seen some apparition. I look down and have to focus to *see* Michael again and remember that he is in front of me and waiting for an answer I can't supply. So I shrug.

"I'm sorry. I've got nothing. I mean, I wish I could help you. That sucks, with the money. And I won't deny it—yeah, we slept together. But you know, it wasn't what you think. We never talked. It was random, senseless, mindless, black hole fucking. I think you know who she was better than I do."

It's Michael's turn to look off-guard. His mouth

forms a little O while he tries to think of something to say, but I just turn around and leave.

I'm back in my room when I remember: unless she quit her job as well, I could find her very easily. I could talk to her right now if I wanted to. She's over at the technical college, being an "assistant dean" or whatever her real position is. I almost pull on my shoes to go ask her what she's trying to pull here, then I think, "Screw it." If she couldn't even leave a one-line note, it means she doesn't want to see me. I'm not happy paying more to cover her portion this month, but I know we'll fill the spot fast, and I'll survive. I'll check my bank account and if things are looking bad, I can always get a little loan from Colin. And if Michael lent her money, he can sort that all out himself. So I call Trisch.

"Hey, it's me. You told me to call you when I got here."

"Oh, hey. So you told her?"

"I couldn't."

"Ly..."

"No, I really couldn't because... she left."

"What?"

"She moved out of the apartment over Christmas. She didn't tell me or anyone else and she's simply gone."

"Well, did she leave anything for you?"

"Nothing."

Trisch sighs.

"Be honest. Did you... care about her... at all?"

"No."

"Alright. Then the problem is solved."

23

Strange dayz. Strange dayz.

My room is bare—I stalk down our halls, put on my thickest coat and prowl around the streets in our neighborhood, staring up at the city stars. Salty and hard as crystal. There's been no snow recently, only a chill deep enough to freeze the blood in your veins. The streets are streaked ghostly white like they'd been crying and crunch underfoot from all the sand and rocks thrown down to keep us all from falling, slipping. Sometimes, I walk around all night, just thinking.

Colin is gone and I miss him aimlessly. He's doing a short run down in New York, and I wish I could visit him every weekend, but neither of us have the time right now and I certainly don't have the money.

The apartment makes me restless and I know what this means. I'll have to move again. I sink myself into work at Helena's. I train, doing Pilates, ballet, stretching, moving—trying to get in perfect form for the audition. I don't dare get my hopes up.

As for Valerie, I don't miss her. It's not like we were friends (not really), and I don't wish her back in my life. But there are parts of her that stay in my life, and no amount of wishing will get them to go back out again. Sometimes, I fantasize about marching into the college, going right up to her desk and blurting, "I don't care why you left. I don't care what I meant to you. You don't have to go out with me now, or spend any time with me. But why? That's all I want to know."

I walk.

My lips bust open from the dry, raw winds.

When I dance at Helena's after classes, preparing for the admission panel, I can feel my muscles and bones tense with the new fierceness of expressing some physical emotion I have not recalled feeling before. Testing a new theory—enjoying dancing alone without enjoyment. Do I feel empty?—No, strangely energized, exalted with restlessness—I want to dance in a completely new way, to shake off the enervation. Yeah, I decide I want to reinvent, dance modern with an open head. To move with clairvoyance. Helena watches, the skin tightening over her hollow face as I end and then raise my head to read her furtively, ask for advice—she knows all about my upcoming audition.

"You want me to give you advice?" Helena tip-toes out to me on her rangy legs. "What can I tell you? I'm impressed by your progress and I'm surprised you were able to add such a complex dimension to your dancing—and so suddenly."

"What do you mean?" My brow furrows and she looks away.

"Ly, technically, I've always thought of you as an extremely competent dancer. And as far as expression goes, you convey a lot, but I've felt for a long time that you were perhaps missing something important. It's an imperative emotion, but not one you can learn, only through experience—and now, you have it."

"What is that?"

I'm curious and she steps forward—lightly touches my arm. I think it's the only time Helena and I ever touch.

"Sorrow."

She says nothing more, though I can see in her eyes she wishes we had the kind of relationship where we could talk. But we don't. And I wouldn't know how to tell her anyway.

I want to be touched, to use my body, but in ways I've never considered before. I go to clubs, not ones I'd go to with Colin where you have space, but enormous, anonymous places too crowded to move. People press their bodies into you all over like garbage floating in the polluted sea. I go into the bathroom, so worked up that I consider jerking off on the sticky bathroom floor—stop myself, watching from above, thinking— *gross.* Then I walk out, wash my hands. Face flushed, hopping with some weird pheromones, and guys come over—hey, are you...?

No, get the fuck away from me. I'm really rude, not shy.

I don't want to be liked by anyone.

I wander home, walking all through the city, dressed up, somewhere in Allston when a random stops me on the street.

"Hey, you going to a party?"

"Coming from one," I tell him.

"Want to come party with my friends and me?"

I look at him—he's got a deserted frat-boy face (nice mouth and I wonder what it would be like to get blown by him—to push him against a wall, grip on his thick neck and rail him, uhhhhhhhhhhhhhh—looks straight as an arrow though, so no chance of that happening—or maybe all the chance)—and I have little clue what he wants with me—but I shrug.

He walks me over to this broken bungalow a few streets over with beer bottles trashing the whole porch—bizarre lumps where the lawn would be rise ominously in the snow, and we go inside the house. Four guy versions of him and two girl versions of him sit in a depressing living room with ruined furniture and soft-pumping music. Everyone looks at me like a strange species has come on board—of course—in contrast, they look tame and under good feeding—but then I'm the one looking at them like they're foreigners. Oh, we're all flying, rushing around—you want some, you want to join? And I've never done coke before—I've never done any drugs before—No thanks, I tell them—they want me to drink—I've hardly ever taken a drink—I feel polluted and lonely on the cruddy couch because I'm not doing any of their escapist things—whatdya say your name was? How you spell that? L _ Y—but that's got no vowels! You can't have a name with no vowels! Independently, the two girls start kissing each other and feeling each other next to me, sniggling, while one guy elbows me in the side—hey, you like watching two girls make out? You don't, huh? Not your thing, huh? Ha ha ha dementedly and I've never been so isolated—what turns you on? I don't know what I'm doing here, but I don't leave. They giggle, like now they're really going to tear into me and I roll up off the couch— Hey, leave him alone—the girls are cooing—you're going to make him leave and he didn't even get hiiiiiiiiiii. They've got pinprick eyes—Some guy is snorting right when I turn up the volume—almost make that coke go down the wrong pipe—

I think about how unbelievably empty these people seem to me—but they're not, they can't be; just like her—she only seemed that way, but there was so much inside. Or so much I projected onto her. And I must seem empty to them, unfathomably so. I want to make us happy though. I want us to be friends. Once my hand leaves the dial, the hip-hop blasts the house, shakes it to its slimy foundations and I start to dance—why not—this turns me on, sure—this gets me high: slinky, grindy hip-hop moves. The girls start hooting—more, more! The guys are staring, trying to figure out if I'm a hallucination and I flirt with all the boys then, shamelessly confident—I can be now that I'm dancing. I am protected by the magic barrier of art. They will not be threatened, they will not beat me up, we will not hurt each other—we will all dance, we will put our arms around each other—the house is bursting open with the pounding surf of music absolving us, making us clean—

We dance until the neighbors call the cops.

The next day, I call Colin. I can tell on the phone that the strenuous schedule of matinees, evening shows and after parties are starting to take their toll—but he still sounds cheerful, more so than me.

"Everything OK?" he asks. "You sound kind of down."

"Everything's fine." I'm walking on the night street, talking into my phone, and I take a seat on a curb. There's no snow at all—it's a shimmering, crystal world.

"You took the snow with you," I tell him.

"Yeah, it's been snowing here nonstop. I'm trying to

avoid this cold that's going around the group, trying to make it to the end of the run in one piece. Half of the company has a bad bug. How are things on your end?"

"I'm moving out of my apartment."

"...OK. That's sudden. How come?"

Excuses.

"Oh well. Not really feeling the vibe with these roommates, and then I'm getting shafted with the rent and the heating here. I could get a much better room cheaper. I only took this one back then because I didn't have a lot of options since I couldn't come see the place in person. But now I know Boston better, and I can visit potential places and do some research. Not jump on the first place I find."

Though I sound alright to my own self in my head (as I suspect everyone does to themselves), I've always thought of my voice on the wrong side of high and thin. Not his, though, and in his hot liquid way he says over the phone, "Move into my place."

"What?"

"I'm not going to be back for another three weeks. That should give you enough time to find a new place. I never sublet it because I don't like the thought of a stranger using my things. But you'd be fine, of course."

I arch my back and lay down right there on the sidewalk. Then I see someone coming—I don't care— they can step over my face, so long as they're not a cop wanting to bust me for loitering. The street is like a bed-spread—and I can lie there talking in my outside bed-room.

"I can't just move into your place. I'll want to wear all your clothes. And not take them to the dry cleaners."

He laughs.

"Ly, then do it. I left a spare with my neighbor because she said she'd water the plants every once in a while. I'll call her and tell her your deal. Please don't fight me on this and just do it. You'll have a nice relaxed month while I'm gone."

"And what about when you move back?"

"Let's worry about that when we get there."

I am lucky—a friend of Mike's took Valerie's room and a friend of his girlfriend's takes mine—so I can move out instantly, and the first night at Colin's cozy studio, I touch everything: try on all his clothes. Blast music, dance sweat all over his hardwood floor, look in his cabinets—and try to find flaws. A secret problem with foot fungus? A depraved obsession for Wham? None reveal themselves. Like I already knew it, like I slip between his crisp navy blue sheets, smelling his spiced cologne.

Two weekends later, I'm finally able to visit Colin in New York. The weekends are not a good time for him with the constant shows, but I have the Monday off as well, and he'll have the Monday matinee free. I watch him in each and every performance; I don't even look at any other dancer. Off-Broadway *Cabaret*—hot, hot, hot. During the intermissions and after the show, I hang out with him in the canteen. The dancers and actors are friendly, and I realize just how much I've missed the chaotic, camaradic atmosphere of every show backstage. Glitter, scatter, and so comfortably unglamorous. Colin buys me hot chocolates from the vending machine and introduces me to all his friends. He has a lot of them and there's one dancer—a guy around my age, maybe a year or two older. Disgustingly *very* nice body, the type I've always envied (there's no fat on me and I'm strong, but no amount of training can get me to look as muscular as someone like Colin or this guy). Next to him, I feel even scrawnier than normal. The two of them joke around and my good mood pops. I feel out of their loop again and slightly rebellious with jealousy, thinking, 'Well, he has been down here for a while now, so this kid's probably his show fling...' Why not, after all, we've never set any boundaries regarding monogamy. This is my first time hanging out with him strictly amongst his friends and peers, and I observe his regular insolent self in a new light. He disarms everyone, knowing the exact dimensions of his own effect and I watch him, infatuated and infuriated. But then Colin sees me sulking—it doesn't make him mad. He kisses me in front of everybody. I'm his, they know it. He's not ashamed to be with me, but I'm shamed then. I think, What are you so worried about?

He's not like you, Ly.

Between and after shows, he takes me around Manhattan, and the city dazzles me. Times Square and Central Park are as spectacular as I've ever imagined. I wish we had time to do silly tourist things, like go up on the Empire State Building and promise to meet there again in ten years, but with our limited hours, we spend them in cafés, on the streets, or in any dark corner.

"Come on..." Colin pressures me anywhere—we don't have any privacy because he sleeps on a blowup mattress in a dumpy room he shares with a few other dancers, but since he only needs body storage for the weeks he's here, he didn't bother to try to find a decent place. In his latent rich-boy way, he suggested renting a hotel room for the weekend when I came over, but just thinking of him throwing away all that money got me stressed and I insisted we go normal. So I sleep on the mattress with him at night, letting him play with me, though even the last night, we don't get far.

"Guys, go to sleep!" Karim yells out. One of his friends and roommates for these weeks. "Or do I need to get lost for thirty minutes? You're cruel enough to make me take a walk at two in the morning in two feet of snow to satisfy your lust?!"

"We're going to sleep," Colin mutters.

"It doesn't sound like it. So pipe down."

We hold our breath until hers steadies. I have my back to him, and then I feel Colin's hand trace the bones of my spine down my shirt; touch me everywhere. I pretend to be asleep, thinking: Do not say anything. Do not tell him.

Don't stop. Keep going. I'm dying.

The next day he takes me out to the station.

"I don't wanna go." I grab onto him like I latched onto my ma the first day of grade school and he smiles.

"Soon you'll be coming to shows with me. You're still dancing for Marichka the Tuesday after I come back?"

"Yeah."

"Good." Colin puts his hand in my hair and roffles it. "You really went platinum this time. Am I ever going to see your real hair color?"

"Nobody has, since I was thirteen. I'm not even sure what color it is myself anymore. But if we're still together... this time next year, I'll grow it out for you once. It's probably puke-brown or some boring-horrible color."

"Hey, what's wrong with puke-brown?"

His hair right now is angled-down Brit pop brushing his cut jaw—I run my hands through it—slick and straight.

"Nothing. I wouldn't dye my hair either if it was this straight and sleek and *this* almost black beautiful puke-brown."

He grins—my bus pulls in. I have twenty minutes until departure. We buy a last hot drink—Colin wants me to eat, but it's not going to happen right now, not the way my heart keeps skipping.

Last kiss.

Then he leans close.

"Hey I..."

"Yeah?"

"I just. I wanted to say sorry for last night. Not letting you sleep. I should've let you sleep."

"It's fine..." Colors breaking out all over my face like pustules—every color a new blemish—Don't blush, don't blush, don't blush.

Without a face, without a voice. (*That's how I like it.*)

He waves when the bus pulls away, like he knows me, which I figure makes one of us.

When I was a kid, I didn't just love the movie *Flashdance*. I committed it onto myself as a cinematic Bible (along with the *Thriller* video and *Strictly Ballroom*). I wanted to be Alex—and I used to tape up my feet exactly like her and spend hours in the rec-room downstairs, until I could've been the understudy dancer for "Manhunt" and "Maniac." Sometimes, I forced my family to watch me perform the various songs and my ma thought that it was genius; Russ was convinced I outf-gged Freddy Mercury himself—and maybe I just thought that if I could *dance* beautiful, interesting—one day it would all reconcile into *being*.

Of course, my favorite scene from *Flashdance* was always the last dance Alex has to perform in front of the stodgy board of judges for the prestigious ballet school she is auditioning for. I loved her performance—that song—I loved how she slowly wins over the jaded committee—and my breath always caught when she screws up and has to ask the judges if she may restart the song and do the dance again, from the beginning. But like I told my mom whenever we watched that scene together and mutually fantasized about my own big-break audition: I wasn't going to put my hopes on second chances. If I ever had to dance in a situation that important, I would get it right the first time. Put every nerve of my concentration in it. But hey, maybe everyone's more confident when they're nine.

I think of that scene with not a little irony when I finally step in front of the committee who will be evaluating my possible entrance into the Conservatory. The space is not nearly as imposing as the one used in the movie—and I only have three judges, not a whole panel—but when I position myself and close my eyes, the only conscious thought I have is: there's no restarting. No second chances.

It's not that I'm not nervous. I pace around outside the door before they call me in, like a cat aching to throw up, but once I get to the middle of the floor and the music starts, I know what I have to do and I'm so grateful to be here. I feel joy, not pressure. My mind clears. Some wonderfully blank and benevolent force takes hold of my entire body—*it is nothing but pressure, and you love it.* He was so right. I missed this feeling right before a performance, when you're pushed down, down, down and then the pressure and the nerves burn away and leave you with nothing but the purest, distilled intensity, the rush of performing—

And though I don't get applause à la Alex, the woman who Colin always called Marichka gives me an interesting look as I straighten up from my final pose at the end and thank them for their time—not a smile, but an emphatic nod—then she bends down to write something. The judges tell me to wait in the room next door, and I know that if they let me go today, tell me that I didn't make it, I won't have to torture myself for the rest of my life with, "If only I hadn't made x, y, z mistake." I gave them everything I could and so I will accept the much more mundane explanation of not being good enough.

But I guess I was.

When I step out into the hall where Colin is waiting, I can't pretend, not even for a second. "I got it, I got it, I got it, I got it!" I jump all over him, screaming, and strangely, he starts hitting me. We start punching each other in the hall from excitement—run outside into the snow (it's snowed in all over, an early-February blizzard) and he wrestles me onto the ground. It's like both of us are too excited to express ourselves in a more mature way than punching, kicking and screaming.

"So now what?" I ask him, my face bitten red from the snow. Colin pulls me to my feet and tells me we're going to celebrate. He's ready to drag me through every bar in town. "And tonight, you have an ID, so you're not going to be drinking Sprite." He pulls out several cards, fanning them out like a poker hand. "My friend Dennis got me these—abandoned fake IDs from the bar he works at. I thought these five looked the most like you, so he said that I could have them."

"None of these look like me!" The cards are ridiculous and I'm falling down with laughter.

Colin pulls one out.

"Please use this one. You have to."

I look at the card. The picture could be me, after a five-year rendezvous with Krispy Kreme and straight bourbon. The stats inform me that I'm a resident of Florida; three inches shorter, eighty pounds heavier, my ID will expire in twenty years, and my name is Moe.

Moe Pleasure.

"You've got to be kidding me. No bartender or bouncer in their right mind is going to accept this."

"Yes they will. Just watch."

So we go out that night, Colin and Moe. The first place we go to, I order a cocktail and slip out my ID— slick bar, and Colin's moded to the max—even used to him, I'm staring—we're an interestingly dressed couple: the neo-modernist and the truant school boy who really wants it. The bartender flicks his polished eyes over my ID and shows me all his capped teeth.

"Kid, you've got to be fucking kidding me."

"Come on." Colin slips over. "Today was a very important day in Mr. Pleasure's life. He deserves a drink."

Cappedteeth's eyes lash his chic down and up, liking what they see.

"Blondie's with you?"

"Yeah."

The charm is turned UP—the bartender pours my drink. Apparently, it's on the house. Then he moves away.

"How do you do that?" I ask, staring at the concoction in front of me. This is the first cocktail of my life and it looks intimidating.

"Do what?"

"How do you get anyone to do whatever you want?"

Colin burns his eyes into me like he doesn't know what I'm talking about and first drink be damned, I almost gulp it. He smiles more.

"You better pace yourself, Momo. I don't want to carry you home."

We rotate bar to bar, club to club, uptown, downtown, until Colin's soused and Momo's souseder—the next thing I know, I'm stark naked in his bathroom covered in a blanket, my arms twined around the toilet in a carnal embrace and "fuck me" written on my stomach in pink glitter lipstick with an arrow pointing to a region of my body enigmatically devoid of orifices. I groan and Colin brings me tea, laughing at my wretchedness. The bastard looks like he's never taken a drink in his life.

"I told you to pace yourself last night. But you always want your own way."

"What the... Did you write this dirty message on me?"

"No, it was the two boys who took a liking to you at the... fourth place we were at. Though I don't know how it's humanly possible, I think they were even drunker than you. They were ready to take you home when I came to the rescue. That's when you finally deigned to get into a taxi with me."

Noxious and needy is a dangerous combo. I pick at his words. "What do you mean 'When I came'? Where were you before?" I'm growling, and into the toilet is the wrong direction. Colin steps behind me, taps me on the shoulder.

"Come again?"

I spin around, look up into his face—let him read each word.

"I said 'Where were you?'. Were you with someone else?"

Even I'm surprised by how vicious and random my accusation is. Colin steps back from my mold-hued self and smites me a glare the likes I've never seen before. I am a kitten that's foolishly unsheathed its claws in front of a panther and his benzened voice humbles me further.

"You must be still drunk. So have yourself another puke and come out when you're yourself again. Try to make it into the toilet this time though. I'm not cleaning the bathroom again."

He leaves, closing the door on me, and I put my lips against the porcelain, sinking into the greenish-gray misery born of immoderate drink and self-pity. Thirty minutes later, I feel a tremendous and sudden lift and stagger out into his bedroom. Rank Captain Morgan sloshes low in my veins. Colin's sprawled in bed reading and looks up at me.

"Better?"

I lay down next to him, putting my head on his arm.

"A little. But I really... I don't know why I said that. I didn't mean it."

And he puts a hand on my lower back.

"Ly, have *I* ever given you reason to doubt me?"

An ominous weight lingers on the "I," but this isn't the time for nuance splicing.

"No."

"Alright. Then don't. I gave you your space. That's all."

I gave you your space is how I suspect fancy boys say *I let you screw around.*

I crimson. "I was drunk." Pathetic excuses. "Why didn't you stop me if it bothered you?"

Colin shrugs. "Who said it bothered me? You looked like you were having fun—I stepped in only when it looked like something could happen that you'd regret. But don't make it my fault."

I nod weakly and his voice loses its edge, but he's still scowling.

146

"So about your new room. Did you find anything yet?"

Like promised, I had researched rooms while he'd been gone and found some candidates, but as Colin had said nothing about me moving out once he got back from his show, I let the first few days conveniently slip by without mentioning it. Silently hoping.

Now my soul curls into a little ball.

"Yeah, sorry—I'll be out of your way soon. I have a place lined up. It's kind of far, but a nice big room, in Brookline. Thanks for reminding me. I'm supposed to call them no later than tomorrow, to tell them if I want the room or not. I can move in any day, they told me."

He reaches over to the nightstand and grabs my phone.

"That's great. Then call them right now."

And I feel nauseous again, with contrition this time—*I'm sorry, I'm sorry,* I could cry—*no wonder you already want me out—I know, I shouldn't be so trying, I don't mean to be, it's just that—just that—*

My despairing fingers bumble to find the number in my phone's memory, then Colin's lips torch my cheek.

"Call and tell them you don't want it."

"I don't?"

"Unless you'd rather move out."

"No. No!"

"You don't sound too sure," he teases and I burn up.

"Only because I was sure you wanted me out, but I was hoping that if I didn't bring it up..."

"...I wouldn't notice that you've stained two of my best shirts, didn't clean the kitchen once in the last month, and puked all over my bathroom? I think—" He starts to kiss me and I swoon. "—you're too *messy* to be gay. But whatever you are, I've accepted it. So call them." He chews my neck gently. "Go on."

And I make the call.

The next week, I talk with Helena at the studio, and we agree that I will keep teaching until mid-March, which is when I'll start at the Conservatory, in their spring semester. I go to each class toeing the air—moonwalking through the days—then there's another pleasant surprise for me: I'm asked to perform one more time in front of a board, to demonstrate a certain level of competence not just in my discipline (contemporary dance), but for ballet and jazz. Though he's really busy with rehearsals, Colin helps me choose and prepare the pieces—later, I get a letter from the school, saying that I will not be required to enter on a probationary basis, but will be entering as a full-fledged student, on a scholarship.

When I tell my mom the news on the phone, she starts to cry. I know she's so happy for me, like I'm so happy and grateful that I could show her some kind of success, after all the classes, and trips, and costumes, and doctor visits, and enforced viewings of "Manhunt" she'd spent so much time on—but I detect a sadness in her too. She knows this means that I belong in Boston now. That I'm not simply taking time off anymore and that when I go back to LA, for the next few years anyway, it will be as a visitor. I tell her about Colin too, that she should not worry because I have an amazing boyfriend who cares for me. And she surprises me because there's no judgment in her tone. She says she is glad, and

I believe her. She wants to meet him next holiday and asks if he would consider spending it with our family.

So I find myself unexpectedly and incredibly happy. And those nights, when I lay in Colin's (well-insulated!) apartment, in his bed, under the covers—when he sleeps and I fit myself next to his perfect body, admiring each muscle, thinking about the class I will teach the next day, or the training I will do the next day, I can say that I've forgotten the white hand coming in the dark. I see it no more and I accept that this happiness is mine, as much as any could be, and for me.

25

We're standing inside the movie theater at Park Place waiting to buy popcorn when Colin touches my arm.

"Hey, look. It's your old roommate."

"Who?"

"Your roommate. Valerie, wasn't that her name?"

He points with his head across the hall while he steps to the front of the line, and my bowels go liquid. I see a girl, her back to me, talking to some guy over by the restrooms. And I don't know, from here, yes, it could be her—it could very well be her. She wears her regular business attire: cowardly, flat, polished shoes—an expensive pea coat—she's on the short side, like I remember. Broad shoulders, lumpy body, slick blonde hair tied in a low knot at the bottom of her neck. Looking at her ponytail gives me a knot, which I feel getting bigger and bigger in my stomach. Malignant bubbles rise, tickle my gorge, and I can tell Colin is looking at me—but then the girl turns to talk to someone who's joined them, and once she is in profile, I can finally exhale. Her eyes are brown, not tinfoil. Her lips are well-painted. This girl is much prettier and knows the proper application of lip-liner. It's not her.

"That's not her," I tell him. He pays the cashier and grabs our popcorn.

"Oh. I could've sworn it was."

"From the back, yeah—I thought it was too."

We show the usher our tickets and step into the theater. It's entirely empty, and we knock around like two beans in the bottom of a can—where should we sit? I jump rows with him, then settle into the very middle and take off my coat; and Colin chews a few kernels of popcorn, then turns to me.

"Ly, uhm, so. Can I ask you a weird question?"

I nod, still shaken from having thought I'd seen Valerie and rather distracted. I take some popcorn too, though my stomach feels peptic and seditious.

"You won't get mad?" he asks.

Uh oh, he wants to talk about something serious. I turn to him. "What is it?"

He can't seem to get himself to look at me, which is odd for him. I watch his dark eyes shutter nervously under their curtain of lashes.

"This is going to sound mildly psychotic, but it's been bothering me for a while so I'm just going to get it off my chest. Did something... ever happen... between you and your roommate?"

"Like what?" Terrifying, how effortlessly I can fake confusion. I put on my best nonchalant face and I guess I'm good, because he blushes to hell and turns away.

"Forget it, forget it. I'm sorry."

"No, no, no, I can't forget it. You think, that what?"

"Please, just forget it. I knew I was being crazy, and I shouldn't have asked."

"Sorry, but you brought it up, so now I want to know."

"I don't know!" He sounds pissed off, because I won't let him graciously back out of this corner, and I feel immense guilt for doing this to him—because he's right of course, but I need to eradicate all doubt in him, as that might be the first step to eradicating all doubt in me. If nobody tells a story, dances a dance, it is denied—*and then it dies.* You force the ending.

"OK," he continues, his voice low and rapid. "I'll tell you. Remember that night, when we were watching the game at your place after we went shopping? And your roommate Valerie came in and said she was going to bed? I don't know what it was, something about the way she looked at you... I told you then that night, it seemed like she was really attracted to you, and I didn't think it was mutual at all, but I don't know. It's like, I felt some kind of *force* between you two and it made me jealous. And then there was that night when you asked me if I had ever slept with a girl—I remember, I was *so sure* that you were going to confess to me that you had slept with her or something along those lines—and then when you didn't, I felt so relieved and, I tried to forget it. And telling you now, I feel more and more idiotic, but when you got her that Christmas present. The pajamas. I know, it's not like it was lingerie, but it still seemed like a strangely intimate gift... and it made me think..."

He talks like a glacier has melted in him. I grip his hand.

"But Colin..."

"Ly. This isn't the place to have this conversation, but I started it, so I'll finish. I know—this will sound conceited, but well. I've never had problems getting anyone I wanted..."

"Because you're one of those guys who exudes lust," I mutter absently.

"Repeat?"

Sometimes, I am very grateful for his condition.

"Nothing, sorry. Go on."

"I mean... I didn't—I don't have problems like that. I've slept with... so many people over the years, because it was easy—and I figured, everybody does anyway. But when I met you— I'll tell you that the first thing I noticed about you was how you moved. You always danced in front of those kids like you were dancing in the MET. But the second thing I noticed right away was that—that you were hot—but you weren't easy."

My face is approaching an unprecedented blush. I lower it into the popcorn and he keeps talking.

"I saw you and I wanted to help you get out of that studio, but that's not all, of course. I wanted *you*, and I could tell you wanted me, and I took it for granted that we would get physically involved, and that while we may become friends, you'd also just be a fuck.

"But I was taken off guard, because the more I got

to know you, the more I saw that you were... not about that. And that was just, so not what I was used to, and it made me want to get closer to you all the more. I know I never said any of this before—I'm only telling you so you understand why I even brought this thing up with your old roommate. Why it bothers me at all. Because it makes me feel like some basic understanding I had about you and us is ...wrong. Or distorted somehow."

More people have been steadily entering the theater. A party of three sits in the row directly behind us and he lowers his voice.

"Listen, I like that you don't play around, and this is my first relationship where I've been monogamous— where I've *wanted* to be monogamous. But I'm still not a possessive person. If you told me you wanted to sleep with another guy, or even a woman, whatever—of course I could accept it, but there was something about her, I don't know, something so off-putting, that made me think: no. Anybody but her."

Anybody but her.

I have a flash, back to the first moment I ever met Valerie—when I hated everything. And the very next thought: terrible, horrible, but so satisfying.

Perfectly beautifully perfect Colin Alexander Savoy.

Is it actually possible that YOU were jealous—over ME?

I look into him, shocked by his eyes' shadows. The browns move from twilight—to all shades of night's blacks and violets, until I can't look anymore and gently cover them with my hand. Part of it is altruistic, because I want to calm him—part of it is selfish, because I don't want him to see my face nor look at the pain of his any-more—but he takes my hand off. He doesn't want to just hear me say it into his ear—like he is, he needs to see me say it with my entirety.

Our language is visual. Physical.

So I have to lie to him not only with my voice, but with my eyes, my lips. My whole body:

"Colin. Even if I wanted to have sex with a woman, which I don't and never have—I promise. It would NOT be with someone like her."

26

"*No.*"

Colin's come out of the bathroom, and I'm waiting for him in the doorway, wearing the tightest, skinniest jeans on the planet, with legwarmers on the bottom over them—and chucks.

He says, "No. Change. Now."

"Come on. You know I look amazing."

I grin back and he puts on his coat.

"I guess if anyone can pull off this look, it's you."

"I AM *Flashdance.*"

We bundle on hats, scarves, mittens, the works, be-cause these are still frosty times—there's enough snow on the streets to swallow the parking meters in our neighborhood. Entire cars lay entombed with only small strips of upper window showing, like little tiny secret bunkers. We take a nice long walk a few neighborhoods over to hole up at the S____ Café.

I love coming here with Colin, though we don't often. It's not that close to our place, but I came here a lot when I still lived in this neighborhood, and I remember how much I liked spending a morning here, snuggled into their soft, comfy couches, sipping tea.

We both have today off, so we said we'd go have breakfast together and then go out to the Charles. This is an unusually late cold snap and we don't have much time left before the ice will start melting. I lean against Colin on the couch, in the warm café, imagining being with him on the frozen river in a few hours—just him—snow—silence—dancing.

His head is against my neck; he's reading. I have my legs hooked over his knees behind the coffee table, then he disentangles from me and puts his book down.

"I'm going to the bathroom. Will you get me another drink?"

"Sure. Same as before?"

"Yeah. Thanks."

I nod and he stands up and goes into the back. I get up and scan the chalk-scrawled board levitating behind the barista to see what I want. Behind me, the door opens—another customer steps in. Pounds snow off of their shoes. I hear the clomp clomp clomp. The guy behind the counter resists scratching a fresh tattoo on his arm. Looks at me.

"What can I get for you?"

"I'll have a medium Americano and a small chai, I guess."

The barista moves behind the coffee machine—the loud schshshchchs of milk getting steamed echoes around, and I'm counting out my change when I hear a voice behind me. "Ly?"

I already suspect who it is, but then the person punctuates the sound by putting their hands on my hips, rights over my jeans. Thumbs lightly sink into my lower back, and my body melts—a falling over head-to-foot meltdown. I jump into the air, spin around and see then why Colin confused that other girl in the theater with her. The real Valerie is also wearing a pea coat (though this one is grey) and black slacks. Her blonde hair is also sleeked down, caught at the neck. But unlike that girl's pretty, animated face, her features are flat and void.

She looks at me like I'm her root canal bill.

"I thought that was you."

I back away from her until I'm almost sitting on the bar, but she seems as casual as ever.

"You look good." Valerie gives me the once-over in that unselfconscious way she has, and I nervously fingle my belt.

"Uhh, uhhm. So do you. So what are you doing here in the old neighborhood?"

Before she can answer, the barista calls over. "The regular, Val?"

My eyebrows raise. "'Val'? What, they *know* you here?"

She tips her head towards the window. "I live just down the street now, at Union Square, so I come in here almost every day."

"Oh. I see." She doesn't say a word about her sudden exit from our old place, so I figure, I shouldn't say anything about it either. "And, work is good? You're still... assistant-deaning?"

"Sure. Work is nothing new, but this new place I have is really something. I'm sharing it with this guy now. Well, my boyfriend, and I think this time he might really be the one."

"Oh?" I'm only trying to be polite, but she launches right in.

"Yeah. Well, I think you'd be surprised if you met him. He's a lot older than what I normally go for, but a mature type for once—has a Bruce Willis feel to him; and you know, it really *is* a small world, but his father and my dad used to golf at the same country club over by Amherst, and he's a regional manager at the same company where my cousin Pete was..."

Blah blah blah blah blah. Oh yeah, I'm thinking, *this is her alright.* The same old Valerie, the same old horseshit—the same old country clubs, marriage gambits, movie star look-alikes, assistant dean—I let her monologue roll over me while I wonder, are you really in a great relationship, or have you found another lug to show off in public while you cry at home? Are you even an assistant dean, or do you wear this pea coat *costume* to fool people?

And most importantly—

"And that's it," she finishes. "That's my life and that's my guy."

I stand still, staring.

I know I need to leave this alone—that I can't know anything about her, perhaps never can, but the acid rises in my mouth, like when my stomach is feeling extra bad—the kind of acid that is even worse than throwing up, because it won't *come up*—won't get out of you—

The barista calls out behind us.

"Large nonfat latte with an extra shot."

Valerie reaches over me and takes her drink, and her eyes are so dull then—like hubcaps—like dulled shards of a knife. I swallow wanting to wrench them out of her face, like maybe if I looked behind them, if I fingered the bare slick sockets *(like you did)*, I could finally know what or who she is. But I won't ever have that satisfaction, so instead I screw her slow and comfortable with a smile.

"Your new man sounds really great. I just hope he treats you better than your last one."

She falters for a moment—that's all I can do. Raze her calm for a beat, as petty as that is, and she takes her drink and steps back. Her dead gray eyes are military, and her smile is a taut, athletic smack across my face that says, *You don't get to tell me what to do. You will never get the best of me.*

Calm and sardonic—

"He will treat me better, Ly. You see, *unlike* my last one, this guy isn't a hollow faggot. So take care. I'll see you around."

I stand there stunned while more drinks are bawled out.

"Medium Americano."

"Small chai."

Colin strides out of the bathroom stage right just as Valerie exits the café stage center.

I know that he didn't see her. I know that I can still have everything if I obediently sit back down with him, where I want to be; that everything can be perfect because we speak the same—(there is no movement that is—)

Go sit down, please go sit down, but—

"Valerie!"

I throw the door open and yell after her. She's walking away as fast as she can, as fast as anyone can on these super-slick streets with the snow banks piled up all around and nothing but treacherous icy labyrinths to navigate through. Her movements are comically ungraceful. I could catch up to her in three bounds, but all I do is call out again.

"Hey, Valerie! What the hell? You never said anything... You just left! You never even said goodbye. Never tried to explain what you were doing with me... Why you were getting into bed with me... why you were fucking with me— Hey—*VALERIY!*"

That makes her stop. Like I'd shot her. She turns around. Her eyes aren't military anymore, they're puffy; her whole face is puffy and she's crying. Not those gentle, bored tears she ignored so easily when she told me about breaking up with Robert. These tears are gangrene; shards of glass carving paths down her skin and she screams at me then, *projectile—*

"No, Ly! You will NOT say my name like that ever again!"

Like you love me.

Valerie throws her latte not quite at me, but at the car nearest to me. I don't know if she intentionally misses or if it's her bad eyesight. The cup bashes against the window—the lid flies off—hot liquid slashes out, cracking the windshield's carapace of ice—a few drops spatter in front of me, brown, sickly blood or diarrhea. The whole world stops to stare at us—(*attention whore*)—Colin has come out of the café; for all I know, he's been standing there for minutes now, watching this whole disintegration. His voice rings behind me as he closes the distance, "What the hell is going on?" and I know then, this dance has no ending—I will never know it—I turn to him, fall against his shoulder, shuddering and

About the author

Ryszard Merey is originally from Hungary and now lives in Germany with his family. He is a writer, illustrator, book designer, ex-mannequin and future kooky old man. His favorite shape is the hexagon.

About the press

tRaum Books is a tiny press dedicated to unconventional formats, with a focus on queer and trans narratives. You can visit us online at http://www.traumbooks.com

A warm thank you

to Dale Stromberg, for his tireless edits and patience with my projects. And Marnie, for being the first reader of this story. I'm grateful to you both.

Further thanks to:
Dermitzel
Brak
Jun Nozaki
Leon Sorensen
Clacks
Agnes Merey
Gele Croom
Philip O'Loughlin
Steven Askew
Tucker Lieberman
Lachelle Seville
Anna Otto

Your support is seen, felt, and appreciated.
Because of you, we can continue to put out the books
we believe in. If you'd like to support our press as well,
you can find us over at
https://www.patreon.com/tRaumbooks.